Telling

(Three plays based on events of the 1921 Tulsa Race Riot)

VOLUME I

"THE GRIFFINS"

"GREENWOOD"

"GURLEY'S GLORIUS GREENWOOD...GONE"

by Dr. Rodney L. Clark

Foreword by James O. Goodwin

RLSC COMPANY

TULSA, OKLAHOMA

rodlclark@aol.com

ISBN   9781796452457   Printed in the U.S.A.   #RLSC014

MUSIC USE NOTE

Licensees are solely responsible for obtaining formal written permission from copyright owners to use copyrighted music in the performance of these plays and are strongly encouraged to do so. If no such permission is obtained by the licensee, the licensee must use only original music that the licensee owns or controls. Licensees are solely responsible and liable for all music clearances and shall indemnify the copyright owners of the play and their licensee agent, RLSC Company, against any costs, expenses, losses and liabilities arising from the use of music by licensees.

IMPORTANT BILLING AND CREDIT REQUIREMENTS

All producers of *THE GRIFFINS, GREENWOOD and GURLEY'S GLORIOUS GREENWOOD...GONE* must give credit to the Author of the Plays in all programs distributed in connection with performances of the Plays, and in all instances in which the titles of the Plays appear for the purposes of advertising, publicizing or otherwise exploiting the Plays and/or productions. The name of Author *must* appear on a separate line on which no other name appears, immediately following the title and *must* appear in size of type not less than fifty percent of the size of the title page.

TABLE OF CONTENTS

FOREWORD

THE GREENWOOD TRILOGY

by James O. Goodwin

Once upon a time, the Greenwood District of Tulsa was the hub of black commerce throughout the United States. It was famous for its cultural and financial achievements, rivaling New York City as a national center of urban black life. On May 31,1921 and in the next two days following, it was destroyed by a well-armed white mob, some of them deputized by the police department. Then, it was the only American city bombed from the air.

Thirty-six square blocks were, razed. More than 3,000 homes burned to the ground. As many as 300 people were killed, many of whom were buried in mass graves or simply dumped anonymously into the Arkansas River. In all, 191 businesses, a junior high school, several churches, and the only hospital in the area were destroyed. The Red Cross reported that 1,250 homes were burned and another 215 looted. Of the 15,000 people living in the Greenwood District, 10,000 were made homeless after the killing and rage ended. Over the next year, local citizens filed more than US $25 million in claims in today's dollars. A former Mayor, Judge Loyal J. Martin, the chair of the emergency committee, declared:

> *Tulsa can only redeem herself from the countrywide shame and humiliation into which she is today plunged by complete restitution and rehabilitation of the destroyed black belt. The rest of the United States must know that the real citizenship of Tulsa weeps at this unspeakable crime and will make good the damage, so far as it can be done, to the last penny.*

In the end, not a single penny was paid to those who suffered the losses because the insurance companies, adopted in court the more palpable view that the mayhem was a "riot", an event specifically excluded from its insurance policies and their view prevailed in the courts. Fortunately, although almost one-hundred years late, the 1921 terrorist attacks are now characterized for what they were- "a massacre". Notwithstanding, the people of Greenwood rebuilt and restored their economy.

But the real story of Greenwood cannot be told without telling the history of the Indian Renewal Act and the Indian Allotment Act. The history involving those U. S. government Acts and the relocation of both Indians and slaves to Oklahoma territory must be included. To understand Greenwood and how it became an economic dynamo is to look back before statehood.

Tulsa geographically is divided by three Native American Nations: the Cherokees to the north of the 412 highways, the Osage on the Northeast of Osage County, the Muscogee Creek Nation south 412 highways. The old Tulsa Country Club in Gilcrease Hills sits at the intersection of all three tribes. Greenwood sits within the jurisdiction of both the Cherokee and Creek Nation territories. The majority of Greenwood is founded on Cherokee Indian territory by blood allotments. The very southern part of Greenwood is in the Creek Nation where Greenwood and Archer are situated and are a part of the original Tulsa township.

With the advent of oil and gas exploration, many residents were reaping unheard of income from royalties. Much of that income helped fund education, startup businesses and created a level of economic independence. At one time, black Americans owned over two million acres of land in Oklahoma. Many spent their money in Tulsa because segregation would not permit them to spend it elsewhere except in places other black Americans lived. The circumstances which gave rise to that prosperity in the Greenwood District in 1921 and the forty years that followed no longer exists but the possibilities for economic prosperity for African Americans and others abound.

Dr. Rodney L. Clark's three plays bring to life the pain, the anger, and the despair of a people who lived through the bloodshed of Tulsa in 1921, and through the horror of it all hope is kept alive. Even today the resilience of the people of Greenwood is being put to the test again but this time under the "color" of the law.

James O. Goodwin has been an integral part of the Tulsa, Oklahoma community and spent his life in service to law, public health and publishing. Born in 1939, Goodwin is currently an attorney at law at Goodwin & Goodwin and publisher of The Oklahoma Eagle newspaper. Recently, the Tulsa Health Department honored Goodwin for a remarkable 50 years of service to the Tulsa City-County Board of Health. In 2003, he received a Lifetime Excellence Award and THD's East Regional Health Center was renamed the James O. Goodwin Health Center.

INTRODUCTION

These fictional characters became "real people" for me as I heard their voices and concerns. I attempted to write down as much as I could to tell their story which is also, my story.

I would like to thank God for giving me the creativity, strength and love for writing stories and putting together this first of four volumes to tell the triumphs and heartaches of the lives of my family, friends and community. As a descendant of the 1921 Tulsa Race Riot/Massacre, I know it is important to tell our story from a perspective that is frequently not heard and often misunderstood. So, I tell these three stories in play form that characterize real people during actual historical events.

I would like to thank my wife Sheila for allowing me the chance to dream and supporting those dreams whether or not they become reality or die. Sheila has been the major cheerleader in my life. I don't know how many times I would write a scene, share it with her and her input would send me back to the drawing board. Sheila deserves much of the credit for keeping me on point with history by making me defend everything possible relating to historical accuracy.

Speaking of staying accurate with the pains of history, I would also like to thank Maybelle Wallace, Carolyn Fulbright, Jerome Jones, Lee Roach, Nora Cruell, Pam English, Lynne Logan, Britni Logan, Monica Bell, Mechelle Brown, Sharon Louie, Jim Goodwin, Emily Warner and Keith Jemison who tirelessly attended readings of the plays and offered constructive criticism and keen insight.

I would also like to thank people in my family and friends who I spoke to for hours about these events that included my Grandmother Leaudra Chaney, my mother Beverley Clark, my uncle Bud "James" Clark, my aunt Sheila Virginia Clark, my cousin Kaye Malone, my cousin Edwina Taylor, and friends and associates Maybelle Wallace, James O Goodwin, and Eli Grayson.

I also appreciate those readers that included JoAnn Gilford, Orisabiyi Williams, Sheila Clark, J. Kavin Ross and James O. Goodwin who read all three plays and offered new ideas and concepts to prepare for the next volume. Kudos to Rita Duncan for her meticulous eyes as she caught little yet very important details to make this book complete. Hopefully, more readers of this volume will share information and feelings to prepare me for this saga of writing a total of twelve plays about the lives of African-American people of Tulsa Oklahoma from 1921 until the future as God sees it.

Telling our stories is something that as African-Americans in Tulsa we rarely do. So, I embark on a new journey to tell the stories of my people from a perspective that I hope many will understand and enjoy.

GRIFFINS CAST

The Griffins is slated for production with Theatre North in Tulsa, Oklahoma at the Tulsa Performing Arts Center on May 31, June 1 and 2, 2019 with the following cast and production crew:

Daddy...John D. Davis

Mama...SynCeerae Robbins

Herman..Dion Berryhill

Leigh...Britni Logan

Isaiah...Ernest Kellum

Margaret...Taylor Horner

Thelma...Ken'Lisha Page

Delma...Terreal Galloway

Robert..Kendell Page

Mildred...Eva Turner

Inspired by God

STORY ONE

THE GRIFFINS

CHARACTERS

DADDY (ALEX) 45-55-year-old male who is the head of the Griffin family. He is a shoe shop repair owner who looks out for his family.

MAMA (MATTIE) 40-45-year-old female who is a mother of eight children. She is also a seamstress who owns her business.

HERMAN GRIFFIN 25-year-old is the eldest Griffin son and is a barber.

ISAIAH GRIFFIN 23-year-old second eldest son who works with Daddy in the shoe shop.

LEIGH GRIFFIN 20-year-old eldest daughter and works with Mama in the seamstress shop.

MARGARET GRIFFIN 18-year-old who works as a maid but hopes to go to college to become a teacher.

DELMA (SON) GRIFFIN 15-year-old fraternal twin to Thelma who is a high school student who wants to play football.

THELMA (SIS) GRIFFIN 15-year-old fraternal twin to Delma who is a high school student who wants to be a nurse.

ROBERT GRIFFIN 12-year-old son who follows behind his brother Delma

MILDRED GRIFFIN 9-year-old daughter who likes to sing and follows behind her sister Thelma.

WHITE MAN #1

WHITE MAN #2

WHITE MAN #3, #4 AND #5 ARE VOICE OVER ONLY

SETTING

The Griffin home in Tulsa, Oklahoma in the early summer of 1921.

Act 1

Scene 1: Saturday, May 28, 1921 - Morning

Scene 2: May 31, 1921 – 4:00 p.m.

Scene 3: May 31, 1921 – 5:00 p.m.

Scene 4: May 31, 1921 – 5:00 p.m.

Scene 5: May 31, 1921 8:00 p.m.

Act 2

Scene 1: May 31, 1921 – 9:00 p.m.

Scene 2: May 31, 1921 - 11:00 p.m.

Scene 3: June 1, 1921 - 1:00 a.m.

Scene 4: June 1, 1921 – 1:30 a.m.

Scene 5: Curtain Call

ACT I

Scene One

(Tulsa, Oklahoma Saturday, May 28, 1921 in the morning. There is sofa slightly stage left in the middle of the room. There is an arm chair next to the sofa. The modest dining room table sits stage right and is draped by ten chairs. Drapes cover the window upstage right. There are also two door openings stage right. One of the door openings is to the kitchen and the other opening is to the bedrooms. On the downstage left side is the front door. In the upstage left corner is another door that is Daddy and Mama's bedroom.)

(The lights rise on the Griffin family sitting at the table eating breakfast. **DADDY (ALEX)** *is sitting upstage at the head of the table.* **HERMAN** *sits to the right of* **DADDY** *and* **ISAIAH** *sits next to* **HERMAN**. *Next to* **ISAIAH** *sits* **DELMA** *and* **ROBERT** *sits at the corner of the table in an odd chair.* **MAMA (MATTIE)** *is in the downstage chair sitting next to* **MILDRED** *who like* **ROBERT** *sits at the corner of the table. Upstage of* **MILDRED** *is* **THELMA**, *followed by* **MARGARET** *and* **LEIGH**. *The family is finishing breakfast.* **MAMA** *rises and walks towards the kitchen.)*

MAMA. Excuse me Daddy and everyone, I got to get down to the shop. I got a whole lot of sewing to do.

*(**MAMA** exits to the bedroom upstage left.)*

DADDY. Mama you hardly touched your food. I guess you thinking about all the things you need to do. Seems like business is picking up at the seamstress shop.

LEIGH. *(rising)* Yes Daddy! Excuse me. I got to get ready and help her. Mr. Williams' daughter is getting married and Mrs. Williams want us to make eight dresses for Ida's wedding.

DADDY. You talking about Mr. Williams at the Dreamland Theatre's daughter little Ida?

LEIGH. Yes sir! I hope everybody has a good day. I got to get ready.

*(**LEIGH** takes her plate to the kitchen and then enters the hallway where the bedrooms are located.)*

HERMAN. Who is she marrying? Isaiah didn't you used to be sweet on her?

ISAIAH. Hush your mouth Herman. She was always too snobby for me. Whoever marry her will be working for the rest of their lives just to take care of her.

MARGARET. He won't have to worry about nothing. Mr. Williams is going to be a rich man one day. The way folks pack those picture shows, he is sure to be rich.

THELMA. Mildred, you hurry up and eat! I need to get to school. We have a major review in Chemistry and I want to get there early. You too Robert! Hurry up.

ROBERT. But, Son is gon' take me today. He was supposed to show me how to rope calves at Mr. Wilson's place before school starts. Daddy can I go with Son please? I don't want to go with Sis.

DADDY. *(To* **DELMA.***)* Is that right Son?

DELMA. Yes sir! Mr. Wilson say us boys can practice before and after school. He says it is almost time for Rodeo season and if we work hard we might be able to make some good money this summer. He says that if we behave and learn, he might have a job for us. He says Robert can even learn how to take care of the calves.

THELMA. Delma Edward Griffin, why do you always try to get Robert out of going to school on time. He bet not be late for school and you either! To be my twin, you are always doing the opposite of what I do.

DELMA. Thelma Edwina Griffin, I am not trying to keep Robert away from school. And we will not be late for school! All I am trying to do is do what Daddy has always taught us to do and that is make money! We all need to pull our weight around here and Robert is now old enough to make some money. You see how good he did just selling newspapers for the Tulsa Star. Robert is going to be a businessman, just like Daddy and Mama! I don't know what you are going to be!

THELMA. Well, whenever I graduate from Booker T., I am going to college, so I can be a nurse! I think book learning can take you further than just working with your hands.

DADDY. Sis, you quit being sassy! A man got to have both book learning and working with his hands if he is going to survive. Okay, Robert you can go with Son. Just make sure that you don't be late for school.

(**ROBERT** *licks his tongue out at* **THELMA.***)*

THELMA. Yes sir! Can me and Mildred be excused?

DADDY. Yes, you can. Now make sure you listen to the teacher Mildred.

MILDRED. Yes sir!

THELMA. We are going to leave out the back door from the kitchen.

(**THELMA** *and* **MILDRED** *exit to the kitchen.*)

DELMA. May we go too Dad? Mr. Wilson says that after a good breakfast it is time to go to work.

DADDY. Okay Son. Robert, you handle them calves good you hear!

ROBERT. Yes sir, Daddy. I will do my best!

(**DELMA** *and* **ROBERT** *exit out the front door.*)

HERMAN. Excuse me everyone, I got to get down to the barbershop. Saturday is our busiest day. And, it is the day everybody talks about what they did on Thursday, Friday, and what they plan to do tonight. They usually talking about how they going to catch a maid like Margaret and help her spend that money she made all week.

MARGARET. Herman, you know I am not interested in giving no man none of my money unless he's serious about courting. And if he is, he better be talking to me every day of the week, including Thursday.

HERMAN. I'm sorry! I'm sorry! I am just telling you what I hear them boys talking about.

MARGARET. Well, those boys had better grow up and become men and get them a job and learn how to take care of a lady.

DADDY. Okay, Herman. Tell Mr. Carter that I will have his shoes ready tomorrow. The man wears a size 16. I got to make his shoes from scratch. Plus, on top of all that, the man is hard on shoes.

(**MAMA** *enters from the bedroom and kisses* **DADDY** *on the cheek).*

ISAIAH. What made you want to open a shoe shop to make and fix shoes Daddy?

DADDY. Well, son I guess it wasn't something that I planned to do. It just dawned on me one day- like when your Mama started taking in sewing. She never thought it would be something that she could start a business and make a living.

MAMA. No, I didn't. I thought I was going to be working for Ms. Lucy all my life. You should have seen her face when I told her that I was going to quit!

(**LEIGH** *enters from the bedroom with her purse.*)

MARGARET. Tell us how you did it Mama. Sit down Leigh. You got time. I need to practice cause one of these days I can't wait to tell Ms. Ann that I will no longer be her maid.

MAMA. Well, it was a few years after your Daddy was doing pretty good with the shoe shop. I remember when he told me that we were doing pretty good and had saved up enough money. I was at work and I had just gotten through with cleaning up the kitchen and it was time for me to go home. Little Agnes was crying her eyes out because she was in her crib and needed her diaper changed. I could tell cause the smell was so bad I could smell it when I walked into the room. Could you believe Miss Lucy was just sitting there looking at a magazine? She didn't even look up when I walked into the room. She just said "Mattie, Agnes diaper needs changed". I said smell like she does. Her face turned around and she pulled her glasses over her eyes and said, "What you say?" I said, yes ma'am, it sure smell like it does.

MARGARET. *(in anticipation.)* OOOOOOOO! What did she say? What did she say?

MAMA. At first, she didn't say nothing. She just opened her mouth wide and took off them glasses and said. "Well somebody needs to change it!" I said real calmly, they sure do ma'am. Then she said, "And that somebody is you." I said no ma'am. I will not be changing Agnes's diaper anymore. You should have seen her. She turned as red as a red pepper and she screamed and said, "Change that diaper or you can find another place to work." I said yes ma'am, and I turned away. She ran up behind me and grabbed my shoulder and turned me around to face her and said, "Yes ma'am what?" I looked at Miss Lucy and I said I am going to find me another place to work and walked out.

MARGARET. OOOOOOOOOO! I can't wait until I can tell Ms. Ann that! I just want to see her face. Did you ever hear from Ms. Lucy again Mama?

MAMA. No. But, I heard she found another maid. I think Freddie Lou started working for her. But, children it is so different working for yourself. Leigh, with the way things are going, we might have to have Margaret help us soon.

LEIGH. I don't know Mama, I think Margaret likes working for Ms. Ann.

MARGARET. Leigh don't you start!

LEIGH. Girl, you know I am just playing. With all these dresses for Booker T.'s prom, we can use some help before the 1st.

MARGARET. Girl, I got to hurry up and get to work. Ms. Ann will start acting a pure fool if I am late. See y'all later.

(MARGARET leaves out the front door.)

MAMA. Good bye.

DADDY. Take care.

LEIGH. Be careful.

HERMAN. Watch out for them boys looking at you.

(MARGARET laughs as she leaves.)

16

ISAIAH. Bye. Daddy. Why did you want to open a shoe shop?

DADDY. I noticed that everybody needed shoes. I saw that everybody always had to get their shoes fixed sooner or later. And one day I was downtown, and I passed this white man's store who fixed shoes. He was fixing white folks shoes, but if colored folks wanted their shoes fixed they had to go to the back of his store in the alley to give him the shoes. Then, I heard that after he fixed colored folks' shoes, he would charge them double what he charged the white folks. Well, like most folks on Greenwood who was tired of going to the backdoor of the white folks' store, I decided that I could open a shoe store too and stop the white folks from making that money and make it for myself. So, I started fixing shoes and taught myself the business by practicing on folks. After a while, I got real good at it, saved some money and got some equipment and now you see Griffin's Shoe Shop and our motto is-

EVERYONE. Try us once and you will try us twice!

ISAIAH. I appreciate you teaching me the trade. I have learned so much that I wish we could expand and open two shops. You know some other folks have already started two of the same business because they are making a good profit. Between Mama's seamstress business and the shoe shop we make a pretty good living. It's like you and Mama have taught us to learn how to make your own living so you do not have to work for anyone else.

LEIGH. I understand what you mean Isaiah.

ISAIAH. Right. But Daddy, where did you get it from? I mean you and Mama are teaching us, but where did you learn it from? We know Mama's people are the Winns from Oktaha. I know me and Herman had some good summers down there fishing with Uncle Samuel and Uncle Odessa. But, Daddy where are your people from?

*(**DADDY** looks at **MAMA**. She returns the look and raises her eyebrows as he stands.)*

DADDY. Everybody sit down.

*(**DADDY** looks in the kitchen door. He looks to the bedroom.)*

DADDY. *(shouting)* Thelma! Are you up there?

LEIGH. They're gone Daddy. What is it?

DADDY. Okay. What I am about to tell you does not go any further than here. All three of you all are old enough to understand. But, no matter what it should not be repeated for anything do you hear me? Do you hear me?

HERMAN, LEIGH, ISAIAH. *(staggered)* Yes sir.

DADDY. It's a matter of life and death for me and our family. Do you understand?

HERMAN, LEIGH, ISAIAH. *(staggered)* Yes sir.

DADDY. I am from Coldwater, Mississippi. My family members were sharecroppers down there dealing mostly in cotton. I was working with my mom, dad, four brothers and three sisters. I am the oldest son. I was about Herman's age 20 or so when it happened. While coming home in my wagon from town two white guys on horseback stopped me and started harassing me. One of them told me to get off the wagon. Why sir, I asked. He said to shut my mouth and do what he says. So, I got off my wagon and he got off his horse. He hit me real hard across my mouth. It caught me off guard and I fell to the ground. The other white man got off his horse and they both started beating and kicking me. They were throwing me back and forth and beating me until I fell near the wagon. I picked up my gun and I shot one of them in the chest. The other one started running to his horse and I shot him in the back. I was wounded very bad. But, that did not stop me from shooting them both again to make sure they were dead. I gathered myself and I drove my wagon back home to my family. My mother and father names are Herman and Leigh Grier.

LEIGH. Herman and Leigh?

DADDY. That's right. You and Herman were named after them. When I told them what happened, they said I had to leave Coldwater and never come back or the white folks would kill me. That same night my mother and father gave me some supplies. They told me to go far away and never come back or I was sure to be a dead man. So, I never went back. When I was in Louisiana, I heard about Negroes settling in Oklahoma and doing real good for themselves. And on my way through Texas, they were calling Tulsa the promised land for Negroes. So, I came this way and met your Mama in Haskell. Yea. I killed two white men and I don't regret one bit of it. It was either them or me. No. I do not know if I will ever see my family again. And frankly, it has been over 20 years, and I don't know if they are alive or dead. Plus, since I changed my name to Griffin, they will never know where or who I am now.

LEIGH. So, my Daddy killed a white man.

ISAIAH. Two of them.

MAMA. Never to be talked about again.

DADDY. That's right.

(They all look at each other as the lights fade).

End of Scene One

Scene Two

(May 31, 1921 - 4:00 p.m. **MAMA** *and* **LEIGH** *enter the front door.* **MARGARET** *is sitting at the dining room table.* **LEIGH** *and* **MAMA** *are carrying dresses and* **MARGARET** *is drinking a cup of coffee.*

MAMA. *(To Margaret)* Why come you didn't go to work this morning? You know Miss Ann is looking for you.

MARGARET. I set it up yesterday by telling her I didn't feel good. I told her I might not be in today. I was cramping all night.

LEIGH. You know Margaret done got grown quick all of a sudden.

MARGARET. What are you talking about Leigh?

LEIGH. You seem to be calling your own shots. Like you don't care about nobody but you. Even how you seem to always want to join in men folk's business.

MARGARET. I just like to stay informed on what is going on.

MAMA. I don't know Leigh. Sooner or later men folks' business become women folks' business. To be honest with you I don't know what they would do without us.

MARGARET. Right Mama. We need to know what is going on. Half the time, men won't tell us what they go through. Men like Daddy have a hard time expressing their feelings.

MAMA. Naw. You don't know your Daddy like I know him. That man when he makes up his mind about something ain't no turning him around. He can be as stubborn as a mule.

LEIGH. Margaret. How you know about all this stuff?

MARGARET. I read the paper Leigh. When I am at Ms. Ann's I read the Tulsa Tribune as much as I can when Ms. Ann ain't looking. That paper gives me a chance to see what the white folks are thinking and what they're about to do. That paper says some mean stuff about black folks. Stuff that I know ain't true cause I live with Negroes and I know we don't do or say the types of things that paper be saying. And when I get back on the north side of the tracks and on Greenwood, I pick me up a Tulsa Star or a Tulsa Sun and I see what they are saying about what the white folks is saying. I see why Daddy always calling white folk peckerwoods and bad names.

LEIGH. Where you get all this reading stuff from gal?

MARGARET. Booker T.

LEIGH. Oh yea. You were one that always took to them books well. You and Sis have always

19

been pretty good in that area. I know you wished you could go to college, but right now it's a long shot.

MARGARET. That does not stop me from keeping informed. I like to read A.J. Smitherman's paper. The Tulsa Star is good for Negroes who like to read. I picked up a paper after Miss Little did my hair today.

MAMA. What did you find out?

MARGARET. They saying they trying to stop Dick Rowland from being lynched. They say they hope that Negroes in Tulsa join them tonight to go to the courthouse and protect Dick Rowland from the white folks who want him dead. But Smitherman also say that Dick Rowland's situation ain't got nothing to do with what is really going on?

LEIGH. What are you talking about Margaret?

MARGARET. There is an article in the Tulsa Star that says all this new commotion with Dick Rowland is just a cover up for the real conspiracy that is going on with Greenwood.

MAMA. What are you trying to say Margaret?

MARGARET. I am not trying to say anything. J.B. Stradford is the one who wrote the article. He says that Dick Rowland's arrest was a conspiracy.

LEIGH. Really?

MAMA. What if Stradford is saying is really the truth?

MARGARET. Stradford says that white folks know that the elevator incident was staged, and an excuse to get white folks riled up. These white folks in Tulsa want the Greenwood area. They want to move all the Negroes out and expand downtown. Now the Negroes don't want to sell it. But, the white folks want it for themselves.

MAMA. Daddy did say something about that O.W. Gurley was asking Negroes if they would be willing to sell their property on Greenwood. And Daddy wasn't hearing none of it. With the seamstress shop and the Shoe Shop next to each other it would be like we are chopping ourselves off. I agreed that we would be stupid to sell our property.

MARGARET. Stradford even goes as far as saying that some Negroes have already been bought off by the white man. This could be why Daddy is not wanting to listen to O.W. Gurley. Stradford even goes as far to name Sheriff Barney Cleaver may be involved.

LEIGH. Sheriff Cleaver? Ain't he the police for the Negroes? He always call himself trying to keep law and order on Greenwood. The white folks call him all the time and tell him to make sure we don't get to drinking and dancing too much at Odd Fellow's Hall. White folks don't know how classy we are. Some of them be too scared to walk into the Odd

Fellows. They need Sheriff Cleaver and his deputies to handle it, just in case our men folks get too much to drink.

MAMA. Whatever happened to Buster? You talkin' about Odd Fellow's dance hall made me ask you about Buster. Didn't he take you to Odd Fellows last week?

LEIGH. He's still around. Say he was gone be gone for a couple of weeks working on the railroad. He'll be back here after a while. I look for him to come to the dress shop a calling soon. He says he want to meet Daddy at the house. Say he don't want to go to the shoe store and talk to him. He says he want to officially start calling on me here, but you know how Daddy is. Daddy ain't wanting nobody come around here unless he got some money in his pocket and wanting to do something with himself. Bless his heart, ole' Buster call himself want to have something. Say he trying to make enough money on that railroad to open a restaurant on Greenwood. Humph! We will see.

MAMA. Be careful. Sound like you a little sweet on him.

MARGARET. *(looking at the paper.)* OOOoooo! Stradford says some of these Negroes are trying to conspire with these white folks. He is comparing it to how some Africans helped white folks capture their own people. He says Negroes don't need to let white folks buy land on Greenwood. He says white folks are wanting to build close to downtown and Greenwood is proper pickings.

*(**THELMA**, **MILDRED** and **ROBERT** enter the dining room.)*

THELMA. Hi Mama. One more day of school. I've been working hard on my finals. I know I will do well on my Chemistry test tomorrow. Plus, Mr. Woods is talking about starting a football team and a band next year. Booker T is so exciting.

MILDRED. I want to go to Booker T.

MAMA. You will Mildred. First, you got to get out of Dunbar.

LEIGH. Then after that you will go to Carver.

MARGARET. Yes. You will like Carver. Sis, are they going to have cheerleaders and majorettes?

THELMA. I hope so. Mr. Woods say that these activities will be after school. And, we will have to try out. He says if our grades are good we can participate-

*(**DELMA** enters.)*

THELMA. So, I know some people who will not be able to participate.

DELMA. I heard you. Don't worry. I am going to be on the football team.

21

MAMA. You all get on out of here now and do your chores before dinner. Robert tie your shoes boy!

ROBERT. Yes ma'am!

(**THELMA**, **DELMA** *and* **MILDRED** *walk to the bedroom as* **ROBERT** *stops to tie his shoes.*)

ROBERT. Wait for me!

(**ROBERT** *runs out the door downstage right and* **LEIGH** *follows him.*)

MAMA. Margaret. Since you didn't go to work today and did not feel too good, but you got your hair done, looks like you can wash a few clothes around here and do some ironing. You might be able to pull that on Miss Ann, but girl you ain't got time to sit around here and read them newspapers.

MARGARET. But, Mama! I need a day off from all that stuff.

MAMA. If I recall Maid's day off is on Thursday, not Tuesday. You ain't that sick if Miss Little is doing your hair. You know Miss Ann ain't gon' pay you for missing a day.

MARGARET. But, Mama. I really didn't feel too good.

MAMA. I don't feel good everyday either, but I still got to work.

MARGARET. Housework, housework that is all I do. I want to go to college and be somebody successful.

MAMA. You will. You will go to college real soon.

MARGARET. (excited) Really, Mama really?

MAMA. Yes, ma'am. As soon as you save enough money working for Miss Ann to pay for it.

MARGARET. Mama! Okay! I will save a dollar every week and one day I am going to be a teacher or somebody famous!

(**MAMA** *starts to her bedroom.*)

MAMA. Yea, but in the mean time you wash them clothes and iron your Daddy's shirts.

MARGARET. (disappointed) Yes ma'am.

(**MAMA** *exits into her bedroom.* **MARGARET** *picks up the paper and starts reading as* *she exits into the kitchen as the lights fade to black).*

End of Scene Two

Scene Three

(May 31, 1921 at 5:00 p.m. **DADDY** *is sitting in the arm chair. He is working on a shoe.* **HERMAN** *and* **ISAIAH** *enter through the front door.)*

HERMAN. I have told Dick a thousand times if I haven't told him another thousand times to leave that white girl alone.

ISAIAH. You know how Dick is man. He is just crazy about that girl.

HERMAN. But, it just ain't worth it. White girls ain't nothing but trouble.

DADDY. What are you boys talking about?

HERMAN. Daddy, they have accused Dick of trying to rape that white girl that he been seeing.

DADDY. You mean the white girl we saw him talking to in the alley the other day?

ISAIAH. That's the one.

DADDY. I thought Dick would listen to you about messing with them white girls. Ain't he supposed to be your buddy? Maybe he just like taking risks.

HERMAN. I tried to tell him. He said that he really liked the girl. He said they even…. You know….

DADDY. Oh, boy. He done got hooked now. He hooked liked them Negroes is on that corn whiskey!

ISAIAH. But you see Daddy that is not the only situation that we are dealing with here.

DADDY. What is going on?

HERMAN. Supposedly, Dick and Sarah-that's the white girl's name, was on the elevator when it stopped. As the door opened, she screamed, and a white man saw Dick and her, were the only ones on the elevator. The white man claimed Dick tried to rape the girl.

DADDY. I thought you just said he-

HERMAN. He did!

DADDY. Then why did he try to- If he already slept with her, why would he want to rape the girl? That don't make no sense.

HERMAN. Well, Dick said they were just playing around in the elevator and he was tickling

24

her-

DADDY. And she screams out and all hell breaks loose when the elevator opens up and this white man sees a Negro in there with a white girl! I see.

ISAIAH. But Daddy that ain't even the half of it.

(**LEIGH** *enters from the kitchen and starts setting the table.*)

DADDY. Okay. What's the other half?

ISAIAH. Well the police arrested Dick for rape. You know them white folks are going to lynch him. So, some Negro men folks are talking about going down there and telling them to let Dick go.

DADDY. Were they talking about this at the barber shop?

HERMAN. Yes sir! They are trying to get as many men folk together and figure out how to keep Dick from being lynched. And Daddy, I want to go help them.

DADDY. So, you do huh? What are you going to do if the Negroes in this town can't stop it?

HERMAN. I know Daddy, but Dick is my friend. We have got to stop letting these white folks push us around. They're going to lynch him for no reason. It ain't right. It just ain't right!

(**MAMA** *enters from the bedroom.*)

MAMA. What ain't right?

LEIGH. Don't tell us it's about your friend Dick and the trouble folks are talking about with that white girl?

ISAIAH. You know it is. Everybody on Greenwood is talking about it.

MAMA. But Herman, that is not your fight. I don't know how many times you have told Dick to stay away from that girl. He knows the risks involved. He got caught up with her and he needs to deal with his own troubles. It ain't got nothing to do with you or this family. These white folks have their own world and we have ours. Any fool that wants to cross the line and take those types of risks can just do it on their own.

LEIGH. Ms. Dennie came into the shop today to pick up her dress that we let out a notch. The first thing she started talking about was Dick and that girl. What is the girl's name again?

HERMAN. Sarah. Sarah Page.

LEIGH. Yes. Well anyway, Ms. Dennie said she done seen them sneaking around in some weird places. Say they be meeting in places like that elevator where Ms. Sarah work at. You should have heard Ms. Dennie talking about them two. She said people on the North side of the tracks know, but some of them white folks on the South side of the tracks act like they don't have a clue about the two of them fooling around. Ms. Dennie say she know them white folks done seen them together. I know one thing, if that girl don't watch out she could be in some real trouble. Look around and there be another baby in this world that might have to start passing.

MAMA. Stop it now Leigh. You know how Ms. Dennie be gossiping.

LEIGH. Mama. You know everybody in Greenwood know how that shoe shine boy, friend of Herman's, done lost his mind about that white girl. I think he get what he got coming to him. I mean, as many young ladies we have up and down Greenwood and throughout our part of town you would think he could find something that won't get him killed.

HERMAN. Well Dick has always been a free spirit.

LEIGH. The only spirits I know are dead spirits. That's what he's about to be.

HERMAN. I don't care. It just ain't right. They ain't got no business locking him up like that. The next thing they will do is lock me, Isaiah, Delma or anyone else up for nothing. We need to go down there and demand to get him out. Daddy, what do you think?

DADDY. Herman does have a point Mama. There comes a time when you have to stand up for something. If we let these white folks continue to bully us around, they will always treat us like crap. Especially if we don't stand up for ourselves. Calling folks out of their name, saying you can't come to their store, making your price higher than the white man's price for a bottle of milk. I'm telling you to this thing with Dick Rowland has gotten out of hand. At least we can go down there and support him and see what's going on. Herman, who's all going down there and what do they plan to do?

HERMAN. The leaders are supposed to be having a meeting. They said they are supposed to be meeting at the Tulsa Star Office this evening with Stradford, Smitherman, Dr. Bridgewater and anybody else who is concerned about stopping Dick's lynching. In the barbershop they were talking about how they knew that the Tulsa Tribune would print something in the newspaper to stir up the white folks. Smitherman was at the barbershop and he already said he was ready to counter what the Tulsa Tribune printed. He said that the Tulsa Star needed to let colored folks know the real story.

MAMA. Daddy! That boy ain't none of our business. We are doing fine in Tulsa. We have a family. We got eight children who need us to give them the same opportunities we had. The Greenwood district is what most folks call the promised land. This is finally a place where Negroes can go and make a decent living. This is the dream that we both have wanted for so long. Why would you want to give all of that up for a young black boy who done lost his mind over a white girl? Let it go Daddy.

DADDY. Mama that is why it is important for us to support the boy and take a stand. We can't let that white man come in our community and tell us what to do. We got to be examples for our kids and let them know that we stand for something. Plus, Herman didn't you say that all they were going to do is have meeting and decide what to do.

HERMAN. That's all.

MAMA. We need to make sure that everyone is okay and keep a tight knit on our family Daddy. Let's take care of home first. Please.

DADDY. I'm going to take care of home. Don't you worry. But, we also got to make sure that we support each other. Dick needs our help right now. So, what he slept with that white girl! She let him. A man should have the right to live his life the way he wants to. Dick and Herman grew up together. If I was Dick's daddy, I would expect that he would do the same thing for one of my sons. I am going to the meeting tonight to see what is going on for myself. Herman, you can go with me if you like.

HERMAN. Yes, sir Daddy!

ISAIAH. Daddy can I go?

DADDY. No son. I need your help here. If anything happens to me or Herman, you need to be here to help your Mama. You need to step up and learn to be a man. Do you hear me?

ISAIAH. Yes sir.

DADDY. Herman. What time is that meeting?

HERMAN. In about a half-hour.

DADDY. I guess we bets be going?

(**DADDY** and **HERMAN** *walk out the front door as the lights fade.*)

End of Scene Three

Scene Four

(One hour later - 6:00 p.m. **THELMA** *is standing in the living room near the arm chair.* **DELMA**, **ROBERT** *and* **MILDRED** *are standing near the front door in a line as if they are in the choir.* **MAMA**, **LEIGH** *and* **MARGARET** *are sitting at the dining room table watching the children.)*

THELMA. Okay Mildred. Remember you must sing real loud. The church has got to hear you all the way in the back. We will try it again. Remember brothers, you both have to come in with the chorus. Do you get it?

ROBERT. Yes. We got it!

DELMA. Come on Thelma! You just have to boss somebody.

THELMA. Just act right Delma! Mama, tell him to act right!

MAMA. Delma listen to her now. She is the Director.

DELMA. Yes ma'am.

THELMA. *(Directing)* Thank you, Mama! Okay here we go! One, two three!

MILDRED *(singing)*
Jesus loves me this I know
For the bible tells me so
Little ones to him belong
They are weak, but he is strong

(**THELMA** *waves her hands for the boys to join in as she sings with them.)*

DELMA, ROBERT and **THELMA.** *(singing)*
Yes, Jesus loves me
Yes, Jesus loves me
Yes, Jesus loves me
The bible tells me so

THELMA. Again.

MILDRED *(singing)*
Jesus loves me this I know
For the bible tells me so
Little ones to him belong
They are weak, but he is strong

DELMA, ROBERT and **THELMA**
Yes, Jesus loves me
Yes, Jesus loves me
Yes, Jesus loves me
The bible tells me so

THELMA. Good! Okay. We will work on the second verse tomorrow.

MILDRED. So, when will I get to sing it in church?

THELMA. When we have youth choir day on the third Sunday. We need to keep practicing though and there are a few more verses I've got to teach you.

DELMA. Mama, can we go outside and play now?

MAMA. Have you finished your homework?

DELMA. Not yet.

MAMA. Well, I suggest you get to your homework first or you can forget about going outside to play.

THELMA. Mama, I finished mine. I will help Mildred with her time tables though. Come on Mildred.

MAMA. Take Robert with you. From my understanding after talking to his teacher at Bryant's Drug store, he can use all the help he can get.

THELMA. Yes ma'am. Come on Robert.

MAMA. Speaking of teachers. Thelma, I ran into Mr. E.W. Woods at Mann Brothers the other day. He told me that you are a real bright student and Booker T. is happy to have you! You keep working hard young lady. And, Oh, Mr. Delma, Mr. Woods said that you are a good football player.

DELMA. Did he Mama?

MAMA. Yes, he did. He said that the way the coach was talking if you keep working hard, you might even get to start next year.

DELMA. Wow! I am going to work hard you watch!

MAMA. But, he also said that you need to work a little harder in your English class. He said something about you not doing too well on your last English test?

DELMA. I will study harder Mama, I promise.

MAMA. I hope so. Because if we can't do better on our English work football will be over. Do you understand?

DELMA. Yes ma'am.

MAMA. Now, go on in there and do your English homework and show it to me when you get finished.

(DELMA leaves followed by **THELMA, MILDRED** *and* **ROBERT. THELMA** *snickers at* **DELMA.***)*

MAMA. Sis! Leave Son alone!

THELMA. *(exiting)* Yes ma'am.

MARGARET. Boy! They are funny.

*(***DADDY** *and* **HERMAN** *enter through the front door and are followed by* **ISAIAH.** **DADDY** *sits in the arm chair that is empty.* **HERMAN** *stands above the sofa as* **MAMA, MARGARET** *and* **LEIGH** *enter the living room. All eyes focus on* **DADDY.***)*

DADDY. Well them peckerwoods don't know who they are messing with. Negro folks around here, mean business. We ain't allowed one Negro to get lynched in this town and we ain't about to start now.

MARGARET. But Daddy, didn't you read in the newspaper about how they lynched a white man?

DADDY. Hush up now gal! You ain't got no business listening to grown folks talk. You ain't old enough to know what is going on around here.

MAMA. She is working now. You done always said that once folks start paying their way, they grown enough to be grown.

DADDY. Yes. I did say that didn't I. Well, you might be grown enough to listen, but you ain't wise enough to speak. So, hush up and listen to what happened in the meeting.

MARGARET. Yes sir.

DADDY. Like I said them peckerwoods don't know who they are messing with. Most folks feel like we need to protect Dick from getting lynch. They say these white folks done gone crazy. Especially after they lynched one of their own. What they say that white boy's name was?

HERMAN. Roy Belton.

DADDY. That's his name.

MAMA. Why they do that to him?

HERMAN. Remember Mama about a year ago. They say he killed a white taxi driver. White folks were so mad at him that they didn't give him a fair trial.

ISAIAH. Oh yea. I remember that. They say a white mob took him out the county courthouse and the sheriff didn't even try to stop 'em. And when they finally did get to where the mob took Belton it was too late. They done already lynched him.

LEIGH. I remember that. It had Negroes walking on egg shells for a while. They figured if white folks did that to their own, that Negroes wouldn't have a chance if they did something wrong or not.

MAMA. Who was all at the meeting and what did they have to say?

DADDY. Folks like the Mann Brothers, O.W. Gurley, A.J. Smitherman, Dr. Bridgewater, J.H. Goodwin, and some of the other business owners on Greenwood. Old Bridgewater say that this community has been keeping Negroes from getting lynched all this time and it don't make no sense in letting it get started. And I am with him!

LEIGH. So, Daddy what are they going to do?

DADDY. We gon' stand up for the boy! He ain't done nothing!

MAMA. Oh Daddy! Ain't no telling what is going to happen. Those white folks might try to do something crazy!

DADDY. Let 'em. I ain't never been afraid of no peckerwood and I ain't gon' start being afraid of 'em. I know one thing, we can't keep letting them push us around.

MAMA. Seem like somebody in this community would want to keep the peace. A lot of folks keep saying that Dick got it coming to him. He ain't got no business messing with them white girls anyway.

DADDY. You sound like O.W. Gurley. Gurley say, it ain't none of our business and we need to mind our own business.

HERMAN. Yea Mama. Mr. Gurley want us to be more cautious. He wants us to try to outthink the white man. He says we need to beat him at his own game. He figures if we wait this thing out and don't go to the courthouse and act like we don't care and just mind our own business they could let this thing calm down and get back to business as normal. He said if Negroes go down there and cause a ruckus it could be damaging for business. He thinks we should just leave it alone.

MAMA. Sounds like Gurley got some sense.

DADDY. All Gurley is thinking about is fattening his pockets. He ain't got no morals. He don't believe in standing up for what is right and what is wrong. See I agree with Smitherman and his newspaper. We cannot let this thing slide. All it is going to do is get worse. Now, Smitherman showed us the Tulsa Tribune articles that came out early this evening. He says it was talking about how these white folks would be doing the right thing by lynching that boy. Smitherman say these peckerwoods are getting more evil after reading that stuff in the paper. He says they trying to justify that they need to keep Negroes in their place.

MAMA. Daddy, I understand. I just-I just-

DADDY. You just what woman?

MAMA. I love you Daddy. And I don't want you or nobody in this family to get hurt that's all.

DADDY. I know you don't. Don't nobody want to get hurt. But there comes a time when a Negro must be a true Negro. Them Negroes who want to keep bowing down to the white man, and be his slaves can keep being slaves. I don't have to depend on that white man to put food on my table. I don't have to worry about him coming to my house and trying to tell me what to do. All I need for him to do is stay on his side of the tracks and I am damn sho' gon' stay on mine. Now if that white girl from Missouri wants to come over her and mess with our colored boys, then that's her business, and his. They ain't bothering nobody. Them peckerwoods ain't got no right coming over here and taking that boy to jail.

MAMA. Well, what did they decide to do?

HERMAN. For one thing Mama, not too many of the folks at the meeting was listening to Gurley. As a matter of fact, most of them like Smitherman's idea.

LEIGH. And what was Smitherman talking about doing?

DADDY. Well. He felt like he had to print something in the Tulsa Star, so Negro folks will know what the truth in this situation. He's already printed a bunch of articles that are against lynching colored folks. And I agree with Bridgewater, "since ain't no Negro been lynched in Tulsa, then they don't need to start right now."

MARGARET. I read that stuff he's talking about in the Tulsa Star.

DADDY. Girl. I can't get you to keep your mouth shut for nothing can I?

MARGARET. Sorry Daddy.

DADDY. No. No. This time you go ahead. I got to let you grow up. Tell us what you been reading in the Negro papers.

MARGARET. Well, I remember reading that determined and armed Negro men stopped the lynching of Negro men in Muskogee, Dewey, Tulsa and a few more places. Seems like they were saying that even though white folks lynched one of their own, they wanted to make sure Negroes never got lynched in Tulsa. And, they were really pointing out that in all cases, the Negroes who stopped the lynching's were armed, and the white folks left them alone. Is that what the plan is going to be with Dick Rowland Daddy?

DADDY. Margaret, you are right!

MAMA. So, do you plan to join them and go down there with rifles and guns?

DADDY. If that is what it takes? I sure will. Herman is old enough. He can go with us. Isaiah-

ISAIAH. Yes sir.

DADDY. Stay here and watch the family?

LEIGH. So, Daddy, when is this all supposed to happen?

DADDY. About 8:00 right after dinner. We're meeting at the Tulsa Star. Herman, Isaiah, go in that kitchen and get my rifles cleaned up.

HERMAN and ISAIAH. Yes sir.

(They both go towards the kitchen and MAMA looks at DADDY who looks back at her as the light fade.)

End of Scene Four

Scene Five

*(May 31, 1921 – 8:00 p.m. The **GRIFFIN FAMILY** is sitting at the dining room table. There are scraps of food leftover, but it is **obvious** that everyone is through eating. Everyone is sitting at their normal spots including **MAMA** who sits opposite **DADDY** at the end of the table.)*

DADDY. Sis I am glad you want to be a nurse. You keep making A's in chemistry and you are well on your way.

THELMA. Thanks Daddy!

DADDY. Sis and Son, why don't y'all take the little ones outside on the back porch and play for a while. It's time for us to have a grown folk's conversation.

DELMA. Ah Daddy! Can I stay! I will be 16 in July. I want to hear about what y'all talking about. Y'all gone be talking about Dick Rowland? Everybody knows about it. They were talking about it at school.

MILDRED. Who is Dick Rowland?

DADDY. Hush your mouth boy! Unless you want my fist to meet your lip! Go on now! Take your brother with you. Children ain't got no business listening to grown folk's conversations. When you start pulling your weight around here, I will let you listen. And that ain't now! Go on now and take your brother with you!

DELMA. Yes sir.

*(**THELMA**, **MILDRED**, and **ROBERT** leave out to the kitchen as **DADDY** walks over to the living room. **DELMA** slowly walks to the kitchen. His shadow is seen standing behind the door as he waits offstage in the kitchen. **DADDY** takes out his pipe and takes a puff. **MAMA** follows **DADDY** to the chair and starts massaging his shoulders. **LEIGH**, **MARGARET** and **ISAIAH** sit on the sofa as **HERMAN** stands above the stage left side of the sofa.)*

DADDY. Well, I guess you probably already know the way folks been talking and carrying on.

MAMA. Me and Leigh saw O.W. Gurley go into the shoe shop this afternoon.

DADDY. Yes. He trying to convince us Negroes to go about this thing a different way. But, I don't care what Gurley say. If we don't stand up for ourselves ain't nobody going to stand up for us.

MAMA. Maybe he just don't want nobody to get hurt. You know a bunch of Negroes with

34

guns ain't a good thing around white folks.

DADDY. Yea, them white folks got something going on too. I just don't trust em'. Gurley can make all the deals in the world with them peckerwoods, but I ain't never knowed a white man, who I would call a friend, let alone a business associate. Like I told Gurley the last time, he came to my shop I ain't got no reason to sell my property to the white man.

ISAIAH. You know Daddy, Gurley is a businessman. He started Greenwood and made it what it is today. Right now, he got a lot of money and I can see where he wants to make a lot more money.

HERMAN. Yea Isaiah, but at what price?

ISAIAH. Don't worry, I'm with you, Herman. Dick Rowland could be me, you, Daddy and even Son. We got to protect who we are and what we already have.

DADDY. Everybody supposed to meet at the Tulsa Star Office at 8:30. We are going to have one more meeting and then if enough of us agree we are supposed to meet at the courthouse at 9:30 to protect Dick Rowland.

MARGARET. Daddy you are not worried about what the white folks is planning?

DADDY. You know something I don't know?

MARGARET. No sir! Now I wished I would have went to Miss Anne's today. They usually put stuff like that in the Tulsa Tribune. They usually are pretty forward about telling white folks what to do and how Negroes are always in the wrong.

*(**DADDY** stands and walks towards the door. He notices **DELMA'S** shadow move, but he does not indicate at all that he saw it.)*

DADDY. What the women folk talking about in the dress shop today?

MAMA. Most of them are worried about what is going to happen.

LEIGH. Mrs. Durant came in today to pick up her new white outfit for church this Sunday. She says Mr. Durant and his boys are talking about going to that courthouse too! She says that Mr. Durant say Negroes got to do right by God to protect what's theirs. But, she talks like Mama though. She don't want nobody to get hurt-especially her kin.

DADDY. Ain't nobody gon' get hurt Mama. We just going down there as a group to help the Sheriff protect the boy. We don't need no white mob acting like they the Ku Klux Klan and lynch the boy. If it was Herman or Isaiah, I would expect these Negroes to do the same for me.

MAMA. I understand Daddy. I've always understood. I've always stood by you and whatever decision you make. You the head of this family. We follow you. I just can't help but worry so. This is one of those times in life that you just don't like it. I don't feel good about it, but I know that it is something you must do. We women folk got to know how important it is to support our men. And I know you Daddy. You will do anything you need to do to protect your family.

DADDY. Everybody hold hands, stand with me and bow your heads.

(They all stand together, hold hands and bow their heads and close their eyes. The family responds as **DADDY** *prays.)*

DADDY. Help us this evening Oh Lord. Keep us strong and keep us safe. Help us to stand up for your righteousness, oh Lord. Help this family help the entire Greenwood community and the city of Tulsa. Let Mama know that we are in your care. Help her to see that you will protect us mighty father as we go to protect our own. We give you all the glory my gracious one. In your son Jesus' name, we pray. Amen

ALL. Amen!

ISAIAH. Do you want me to get the rifles and guns Daddy?

*(***DELMA'S** *shadow leaves the offstage kitchen area as he exits).*

DADDY. Yea. Herman go help him.

HERMAN. Yes sir!

*(***ISAIAH** *and* **HERMAN** *go into the kitchen and get the guns.* **MAMA** *gives* **DADDY** *a long hug).*

DADDY. We gon' be alright Mama. We gon' be alright. Just pray. Just pray.

*(***MAMA** *starts crying and* **LEIGH** *and* **MARGARET** *look at each other and try to hold back the tears.* **ISAIAH** *and* **HERMAN** *walk in with three rifles and a hand gun).*

ISAIAH. Here you go Daddy. I brought all three rifles and the gun. Everything is loaded and ready to go. Here is some extra ammunition, if you need it. Man Daddy! You sure you don't need me to go with you? You know I'm a pretty good shot.

*(***DADDY** *walks over to* **ISAIAH***)*

DADDY. No sir. But, there is one thing I really need you to do Isaiah.

ISAIAH. Sir?

DADDY. I need you to stay home and take care of the rest of the family just in case something happens.

ISAIAH. Yes sir!

DADDY. Now it is important that you do what I say. Do you understand me Isaiah?

ISAIAH. Yes, sir Daddy! Take care of the family.

DADDY. Now you keep this rifle in case you have to use it. Give that pistol to your Mama. I'm going to keep this one, and Herman, I know you like this shotgun.

HERMAN. Thanks Daddy!

DADDY. Margaret, I want you to go to the back porch and tell Son I want to see him. Keep the other children back there for about fifteen minutes.

MARGARET. Okay Daddy.

    *(***MARGARET*** exits into the kitchen.)*

DADDY. Mama make sure everyone stays at home this evening. Just in case we do run into some trouble.

MAMA. Okay Daddy.

DADDY. Herman. I got one more thing to do before we leave. Give me your belt!

HERMAN. What for Daddy?

DADDY. Give me your belt son!

HERMAN. Daddy. You ain't whooped me in years? What did I do?

DADDY. Give me your damn belt!

    *(***HERMAN*** takes off the belt and gives it to ***DADDY***. ***DELMA*** enters from the kitchen).*

DELMA. Daddy you wanted me?

DADDY. Didn't I tell you that you don't need to be listening to grown folk's business? Come on over here boy!

    *(***DELMA*** walks slowly over to ***DADDY***).*

DADDY. Now! Didn't I tell you not be listening in grown folk's business.

DELMA. Yes sir!

DADDY. But you gone listen anyway ain't you boy! Ain't you boy! So, you know you got this ass whopping coming don't you son!

DELMA. *(crying)* Yes sir.

DADDY. HUH! I CAN'T HEAR YOU!

DELMA. *(crying and whimpering)* YES SIR!

*(The lights fade as **DADDY** starts whooping **DELMA** in the dark).*

End of Scene Five

END OF ACT I

ACT II

Scene 1

(May 31, 1921 – 9:00 p.m. **DELMA** *is sitting in the living room on the floor sniffling in front of the sofa down left.* **THELMA** *is sitting on the sofa helping* **MILDRED** *with her reading.* **ROBERT** *walks in from the kitchen and goes over to* **DELMA**.

ROBERT. You got a whooping?

DELMA. What does it look like? Leave me alone Robert.

ROBERT. Okay. I didn't do nothing to you.

THELMA. Robert! Leave him alone.

ROBERT. *(teasing)* Delma got a whooping. Delma got a whooping.

THELMA. Robert leave him alone before I tell Daddy and he gives you one.

ROBERT. Okay. I'll stop. I'm sorry Delma. Okay?

(Delma doesn't respond).

MILDRED. Robert leave him alone.

ROBERT. I was just trying to say I'm sorry.

THELMA. *(yawning)* Come on both of y'all. Let's go to bed. I am tired anyway.

MILDRED. *(yawning)* I'm tired too. Come on Robert let's go to bed.

*(***THELMA**, **MILDRED** *and* **ROBERT** *exit stage right to the bedrooms.* **DELMA** *continues to sit on the floor.* **MAMA** *walks in from the bedroom stage left and notices* **DELMA** *sitting on the floor. She sits in the chair).*

MAMA. You know your Daddy loves you, don't you?

DELMA. Yes ma'am. I just. I just. I just been hearing so much about what is going on and I want to know why people are talking so crazy? All day at school kids been talking about the lynching. Thelma know more than I know, she just ain't talking about it. She scared too. Now Daddy and Herman is down on Greenwood to see the lynching.

*(***MAMA** *walks over to the door leading to the bedrooms stage right).*

MAMA. Margaret! Margaret!

MARGARET. *(offstage)* Ma'am? Here I come.

(**MARGARET** *enters*)

MARGARET. Yes Mama?

MAMA. Go check on the little ones and give Thelma a break. Make sure they go to bed and tell Thelma to come here, would you?

MARGARET. Yes ma'am.

(**MARGARET** *exits, and* **MAMA** *sits in the middle of the sofa as* **THELMA** *enters.*)

THELMA. Yes Mama?

MAMA. Come over her baby. Sit next to Mama.

(**THELMA** *sits next to* **MAMA***).*

MAMA. Delma. Sit up here next to me.

(**DELMA** *sits on the other side of* **MAMA***. She hugs them both at the same time.*)

MAMA. My twin babies. Sis and Son. I love you both so much!

THELMA. We love you too Mama.

DELMA. Yes ma'am.

MAMA. I know y'all worried about this Dick Rowland thing. Ain't no telling what you both are hearing at that school.

DELMA. We were talking about it in class today. People was saying some crazy stuff.

MAMA. Crazy stuff huh?

DELMA. I mean some people is saying that Dick Rowland should get lynched for messing with that white girl in the first place.

THELMA. Yea Mama. But some folks on the other side say they should leave them both alone. If they want to be together then that's their business. I'm just tired of people talking about it. That's all we been hearing all day.

MAMA. So, it's all over Booker T. huh?

DELMA. Yes ma'am. They were talking about how Negroes used to get lynched all the time. Mr. T.A. West was even talking about the slaveowner named Willie Lynch and his theory on how to make Negroes jealous of each other.

THELMA. Yea Mama. I had no idea that lynchings was tied to Willie Lynch?

MAMA. What do you mean Thelma?

THELMA. Everybody at school today was whispering about Dick Rowland and how there was going to be a lynching in town tonight. In history class, Mr. West said he would give us the final tomorrow. He says this Dick Rowland situation was a new teaching moment. He said it would allow us to learn about Willie Lynch. He read us this letter that Willie Lynch wrote to slaveowners who were having trouble with their slaves.

MAMA. Willie Lynch letter?

DELMA. Mr. West say that Willie Lynch was a slaveowner in the West Indies.

MAMA. West Indies. What they teaching y'all over there at Booker T?

THELMA. The West Indies. It's in the Caribbean Islands.

DELMA. Yea Mama. It's in the Atlantic Ocean, near the coast of Florida.

MAMA. Ummm. Hmmm.

THELMA. Mr. West say that back in seventeen, seventeen-

DELMA. Seventeen twelve.

THELMA. Seventeen twelve that's right!

DELMA. Hah! I got you that time.

THELMA. Boy be quiet! I was going to get it.

DELMA. But you didn't. Hah!

THELMA. Anyway, Mama in 1712, Willie Lynch wrote this letter and it was all about what slaveowners need to do to control their slaves.

DELMA. He read the letter to us.

THELMA. Then he made us write key points about the letter as he read it again.

DELMA. Then he made the whole class read it together out loud.

THELMA. Mr. West talked about how Willie Lynch told slaveowners to pit the young black man against the old black man.

DELMA. And the letter said to take the young black woman and pit her against the old black woman. He said also pit the dark blacks against the light skin blacks.

THELMA. Then he said pit the black woman against the black man. The whole point was to get Negroes to hate themselves and each other. Yes, Mama the whole point was to get the Negroes to fight each other.

DELMA. But, he said that it was just important for the slaves to trust the white man even more than they trusted each other.

THELMA. Willie Lynch say that if the white slaveowner could do this, then they wouldn't have any more problems with their slaves for 300-400 years. He said that the secret to controlling black slaves was setting them against one another.

MAMA. Mr. West is telling you right.

DELMA. I know Mama. That's why when Daddy was talking about Mr. Gurley wanting one thing, and Mr. Smitherman wanting another, for the Negroes on Greenwood, it reminded me of Willie Lynch.

THELMA. And Mama I see it all the time at school and other places. The light-skinned Negros seem to always get more privileges than the black skinned Negroes. These boys always seem to like the light skinned girls cause they mulatto and think they're pretty. Mama they don't realize that dark-skinned girls are pretty, too.

DELMA. But then Mama he started talking about something that really made me mad. Mr. West was talking about how Willie Lynch was telling them slaveowners how to break male slaves.

THELMA. Yea, yea. He said for the slaveowner to take the most restless nigger, and strip him of his clothes in front of the other remaining male niggers, the female, and the nigger infant, and tar and feather him.

DELMA. Then he said tie each leg to a different horse and face them in opposite directions, set him afire and beat both horses to pull him apart in front of the rest of the niggers.

THELMA. Then Mama, he said the next step was to take a bull whip and beat the remaining nigger males to the point of death, in front of the female and infant.

DELMA. Then he said not to kill him-but put the fear of God in him.

THELMA. Yea, don't kill him, 'cause he could be useful for breeding.

DELMA. Mama that makes me mad just to think about how somebody gon' set a person on fire and then stretch him?

THELMA. He said that by doing this, the Negro woman would not trust the Negro man to take care of the family.

DELMA. Yea Mama. He said that it was more than just a physical thing, but it was psycho, psycho-

THELMA. Psychological. He said psychological was all about the mind.

DELMA. Yea. That' s right. He said it was about controlling the Negros's mind, and making him put more trust in the white man than himself. The sad thing Mama is that Mr. West seems like he is right.

THELMA. Yea Mama. Look at us. This Dick Rowland thing got us taking sides. Colored folks is taking sides against each other.

DELMA. Yea. Daddy is on one side and some of the Negroes are on the other side.

THELMA. That's right Mama. At a time like this we need to be sticking together.

MAMA. Mr. West is right babies.

DELMA. Yes Mama. They're trying to teach us that we are the next generation to make the world a better place. But, Mr. West say we got to open our ears and our minds to understand why we in this situation today. He said people who don't know their history are doomed to repeat it. I just want to know what we need to do Mama? Is Dick Rowland going to be lynched or is Daddy and those Negro men going to be able to stop them. I know I am young, but what can I do to help?

THELMA. It seems like the white folks are still messing with our minds and we are not smart enough to see it. Mr. West said that even some of our leaders would sell us out to the white folks.

DELMA. Mama it seems like the more we learn, the more we see people for what they really are.

MAMA. Well babies book learning is always a good thing, but as you get older you got to understand how life can get you all mixed up. This world of ours is a pretty tough place and there are some evil people out there, but we got to keep believing and praying that God is gon' take care of us no matter what. Now your Daddy and Herman are going out there to stand for justice. We know God is a just God, and we just got to know that whatever his will is, we got to believe it and know that everything is going to be all right. Now don't the two of you fret none. We got a strong family and we gon' stick together.

43

Hold your head up and keep believing in Jesus. Both of y'all about to graduate with a good education in a couple of years. You got your whole lives ahead of you. No matter what you both stay strong. The last day of school is tomorrow, so go to bed and get some rest okay? Now both of y'all give Mama a hug.

THELMA. Thank you, Mama.

DELMA. Thank you, Mama.

(ISAIAH bursts into the front door. He is out of breath.)

ISAIAH. Mama! Mama! Ahhhh Mama, Mama, Mama!

MAMA. Isaiah! What is it!

(MARGARET and LEIGH come out of the bedroom and go into the living room. They walk past DELMA and THELMA who have stopped near the dining room table.).

ISAIAH. Mama, I know Daddy told me to stay home and take care of the family, but I wanted to be there to see what happened. So, I snuck behind them when they went down to the Tulsa Star. I laid back when they drove to the courthouse with about thirty other Negro men. Daddy and Herman were in the back of a somebody's truck. So, I ran down to the courthouse. When I got to the courthouse there were a whole lot of white men there. There were so many white folks I couldn't count. It must have been at least two thousand. When the shooting started I ran. I ran home as fast as I could.

MAMA. Shooting?

LEIGH. Mama we need to find out what is going on. They might be getting ready to lynch that boy!

MAMA. That might be the case Leigh, but we don't need to put ourselves in the midst of no trouble. Your Daddy and Herman are down there.

LEIGH. Yes ma'am. I'm just saying it don't do us no good if we can't see or hear nothing. Let me just go down on Greenwood and see what folks is talking about. I am sure that folks at the Red Wing Cafe know something.

MAMA. Well, I guess it wouldn't hurt. You just stay away from trouble if you see it.

LEIGH. Yes Ma'am.

(LEIGH grabs her purse and walks out the front door.)

MARGARET. Mama we also need to know what them white folks are thinking. Maybe I can go down to Bell and Little Cafe and pick up a Tulsa Tribune. I can be back home in thirty minutes. It is the opposite way Mama and if I hear something we will know what we need to do. Can I go get one Mama? Please?

MAMA. Girl, why do you always have to know what white folks think?

MARGARET. It just gives you an idea of what they're thinking so you can know what their next move will be. You know how Daddy always say you got to be two steps ahead of the white folks. Thirty minutes that's all I need Mama.

MAMA. Hurry up Margaret. Hurry up.

*(**MARGARET** grabs her purse and leaves out the front door. **MAMA** sits in the arm chair. **ISAIAH** walks above the sofa and turns towards **MAMA** and looks at her).*

MAMA. Boy! Didn't your Daddy tell you to stay at home. You already snuck out of here once.

ISAIAH. I know Mama. I just want to go back and see if I can find Herman and Daddy. When folks started shooting the crowd went haywire and I lost them. They might need a little help. I know you want to know they're okay. Mama they were shooting. Let me go see what I can find out.

MAMA. Okay. Now it is 10:00. If you ain't back by 11:00 whomever here is gon' coming looking for you. Hurry now!

DELMA. Mama, do you need us to do something to help? I can run fast to deliver a message to somebody if we need something. Mr. Woods said I am one of the fastest runners in the whole school.

MAMA. Not right now Son. We will see. You just sit still for a while.

*(**MAMA** walks back into the living room with her hand on her forehead. **DELMA** and **THELMA** look at each other as the lights fade).*

End of Scene One

Scene Two

(May 31, 1921 - 11:00 p.m. **MAMA** *is pacing back and forth above the living room sofa.* **DELMA** *and* **THELMA** *are sitting at the dining room table. Noises are heard in the kitchen.* **DELMA** *and* **THELMA** *run to the living room.* **MAMA** *picks up the pistol off the end table and positions herself in the dining room ready to shoot whomever walks in the door. She hears men's voices, but she cannot make them out.* **HERMAN** *has his arm around* **DADDY** *trying to bring him in the door.* **DADDY** *stops moving abruptly as he sees Mama holding the gun and pointing it directly at him. There is a still pause as* **HERMAN** *notices* **MAMA**. *She puts the gun down and helps* **DADDY** *to his normal chair at the table.* **THELMA** *and* **DELMA** *rush over to the dining room).*

MAMA. Oh Lord have mercy!

DADDY. I'm all right. Peckerwood's shotgun put a few pellets in my leg. It'll heal.

THELMA. Daddy you been shot!

DADDY. Yes, Sis. Daddy has been shot. But it ain't as bad as it looks. I am going to be just fine. What y'all doing up?

MAMA. Sis go put some water on the stove and make it boil real hot. Then bring me a big bowl of water.

THELMA. Yes ma'am.

*(***THELMA** *runs into the kitchen.)*

MAMA. Son go get some white rags and towels out of the cupboard.

*(***DELMA** *runs to the bedroom).*

DADDY. *(to* **MAMA***)* It's going to be all right Mama. How come they're not sleep?

MAMA. Herman. Help me put your Daddy's leg in this chair.

*(***HERMAN** *picks up his leg as* **DADDY** *winces in pain.* **THELMA** *enters and sits the bowl of water on the table as* **DELMA** *enters with the towels and sits them next to the bowl.* **MAMA** *tears* **DADDY'S** *pants leg and looks at the wound).*

DADDY. What does it look like?

MAMA. I see four buck shots that got to come out.

DADDY. I told you Herman! He wasn't no good shot. Them buck shots ricocheted off that brick wall.

MAMA. What happened?

DADDY. Well-

DELMA. Wait Daddy! Do me and Thelma need to leave? I don't want to be listening when grown folk's is talking.

DADDY. No, Son. You can stay this time. You might as well hear what happened from the people who were there. This here ain't no second-hand news. So, we left home and was walking on our way towards the Tulsa Star office. Then Ike Wilson met up with us. He said he wanted to make sure he was there when the Negroes stopped Dick Rowland from getting lynched. Just to be on the safe side, he said he hitched up his family in a wagon with goods and supplies and told them to hold up north on Lynn Lane until he got back. Then, O.B. Mann and some of his brothers was coming down the road and we all walked to Greenwood together. By the time we got to the Tulsa Star there were at least thirty Negroes with their rifles and guns. It seemed like Negroes were coming out the woodworks.

*(***DADDY*** winces in pain as **MAMA** starts cleaning his wound).*

MAMA. That hurt huh?

DADDY. Yes, woman that hurt! But, I know you gon' doctor it up pretty good. Wait a minute. Where is everybody?

MAMA. The little babies are sleep. I sent Isaiah to look for you and Herman. Leigh and Margaret went to find out what is going on. Isaiah said that he saw y'all in a crowd and shooting started.

DADDY. I thought I told him to stay here and take care of the family. And, I thought I told you to not let nobody, go nowhere?

DELMA. He didn't listen Daddy. I guess you gon' tear his hide too huh Daddy?

DADDY. Sho' you right! Wait until I see him!

MAMA. When he said y'all got shot I started getting worried. Margaret should be back anytime. She went down to the Bell & Little Cafe to pick up one of the white newspapers. Leigh went to Odd Fellows to see if she could find out anything about the lynching, and I sent Isaiah back out to look for y'all after he snuck out of here earlier. He was the one who said there had been some shooting at the courthouse. Isaiah and Leigh should be here anytime now. I told them, if they not back here, I was gon send whomever was here after them. I'm sorry Daddy, but I was worried about you and

47

Herman.

DADDY. Woman you say you gon' listen to me and then you turn around and you don't. We got to talk!

MAMA. You're right Daddy. I'm sorry.

DADDY. Boy! I tell you-Ahhhhhh!

*(*DADDY *winces with pain as* MAMA *touches a soft spot on his leg as she continues to clean his wound).*

MAMA. So, what happened when you got down to the Tulsa Star?

DADDY. Tell her Herman.

HERMAN. The Negro Deputy Sheriff Barney Cleaver was there, and he said that the white Sherriff McCullough didn't want no trouble. He said they didn't need the colored folks to come up to the courthouse. They said Dick Rowland was in good hands. And then O.W. Gurley got up and said we needed to all just go home and let the white folks deal with Dick Rowland. He said that starting all this commotion was not necessary. But Mr. Smitherman said that it was time for Negroes to stand up for themselves. That's when everybody started clapping and hollering. Then Deputy Cleaver said Sherriff McCullough told him that he had a lot of men to protect Dick Rowland. He said he positioned some of them on the courthouse roof, in the jail, and the whole building, and there was not going to be no lynching under his watch.

DADDY. Now sometimes Cleaver can be all right, but I didn't trust him or Gurley in this situation. You know them peckerwoods wasn't gon' do right! I told them Negros that we needed to go down to that courthouse and see for ourselves.

HERMAN. Deputy Sheriff Cleaver said that he was in contact with McCullough and he didn't want the Negroes to come to the courthouse to try to defend Dick Rowland. But Daddy, Smitherman, the Mann Brothers, Ike Wilson and the rest the Negroes didn't like it. Ike Wilson got all in Gurley's face and told him that them white folks must have promised him some money. And Daddy told Deputy Sheriff Cleaver that he needs to start doing some real policing and start trying to help these young folks like Dick Rowland from being lynched by the white folks.

DADDY. I told Cleaver right in his face that I didn't trust him. So, we walked out of the office and loaded up in cars and drove down to the courthouse. We asked Sheriff McCullough did he need our help and he said no. He assured us that Dick was gone be safe. We saw he had extra help, but it still was quite a few white folks out there who were not in police uniforms. Them peckerwoods seemed like they got mad just because we came to see if the Sheriff needed some help.

HERMAN. So, when Mr. Smitherman and everybody felt like the Sheriff was gon' keep his word we went on back to Greenwood. When we got back to the Tulsa Star office, Smitherman got a phone call. He said that the white mob at the courthouse was getting bigger and bigger.

DADDY. So, we got back in our cars and trucks and went back to the courthouse. Then, when we get out of our cars, we just standing there looking at them and they're looking at us until one of them peckerwoods say, "Nigger what are you doing with that gun? And Joe Mann say, "I'm going to use if I have to." And the peckerwood says, "The hell you will." This fool ass peckerwood gon' try to grab Joe Mann's gun. Understand now, Joe Mann is an ex-soldier, who done fought in the war and this damn fool gon' try to take it from him? He didn't know who he was messing with.

HERMAN. So, the gun goes off and the white man fell dead. And everybody started shooting. It was too many of them, so we had to retreat to our cars. But we killed a lot of white folks. Some Negroes got killed to. By the time we got back to Greenwood Daddy got hit and so I helped him up and that's when we came back home. I put our rifles in the bushes cause I had to help Daddy get out of there. When we left, they were still shooting. James Nails gave us a ride home.

*(**LEIGH** enters through the front door).*

LEIGH. Mama all hell done broke loose.

DADDY. Tell us about it.

LEIGH. Daddy you hurt! Herman, you all right?

HERMAN. I'm O.K. Leigh.

LEIGH. I was walking towards the Red Wing Café, and when I got on Greenwood, I saw Negroes walking towards Pine. Better yet! Negroes was running towards Pine. So, I kept walking south on Greenwood. Negroes was still running the other way. So, I finally saw somebody I knew. It was my classmate, James Minter. I asked James what happened and what's going on? James told me not to go south on Greenwood. I said James you got to tell me why. He said, 'Leigh it's a whole lot of white folks in deep Greenwood and they're killing colored folks like it ain't nothing. James say they even burning buildings and businesses. He said that when he left Gentry, Neely and Vadel's Pool Hall they had already burned half a block. He said they come in there with a machine gun or something just killing colored folks like it wasn't nothing. He begged me not to go down there. Then, he took off towards Pine. Well, I know James. And, I ain't never seem him that scared. So, I turned around and ran back home. Now that I am home we need to figure out what we going to do to survive. Negroes is running scared on Greenwood.

*(**MARGARET** enters through the front door. She has a Tula Tribune newspaper in her hands).*

MARGARET. Mama I got one! I got one! Daddy you and Herman made it back? Thank God. Daddy, what happened to your leg?

DADDY. Don't worry about it. I'm all right. What did you get that you are hollering' about?

MARGARET. Mama let me go to Bell & Little Cafe to get a Tulsa Tribune newspaper. Like I said before, I always read Ms. Ann's paper to see what these white folks is up to. And according to this editorial they are up to no good.

MAMA. What are you talking about Margaret?

MARGARET. Well Mama. This editorial says they got a call for all white folks to meet at the courthouse tonight to lynch Dick Rowland. I wouldn't be surprised if all the white folks in Tulsa who hate black folks showed up at the courthouse tonight.

DADDY. They did. It was more white folks than I ever seen together before.

HERMAN. It sure was. It was white folks all over the place, but we held our own Daddy.

DADDY. We sure did son!

MAMA. What else is they talking about in that paper Margaret?

MARGARET. They say it's high time for them to make an example of the Negroes. They say these Negroes done got uppity and they got Negroes from all over the country coming here, because they think they coming to the promised land. They say it is high time for these Negroes to come down and it is up to the white folks in Tulsa to bring 'em down. They're talking about doing whatever it takes to make these uppity Negroes with businesses, nice houses, jewelry, and nice cars to pay for what they making Tulsa look like. They say these niggers are making them look bad. They say if they will not sell them the land on Greenwood that they would take it!

DADDY. I knew them Negroes like Gurley and y'alls Negro Deputy Sheriff Cleaver was in with them white folks. This stuff ain't about Dick Rowland. This is about them white folks wanting our land. Gurley is so money hungry that he is willing to sell us out. Just like them so called African brothers who sold us out to the white man for slavery. We have got to fight for our survival.

MARGARET. (reading) Daddy, there is also an article in here about Dick Rowland. The title says, "Nab Negro for Attacking a Girl in an Elevator." A negro delivery boy who gave his name to the police as 'Diamond Dick' but who has been identified as Dick Rowland, was arrested on South Greenwood avenue this morning by Officers Carmichael and Pack, charged with attempting to assault a seventeen-year-old white elevator girl in the Drexel building early yesterday. He will be tried in municipal court on a state charge. The girl said she noticed the Negro a few minutes before the attempted assault looking up and down the hallway on the third floor of the Drexel building as if to see if there was anyone in sight but thought nothing of it at the time. A few minutes later he entered the elevator she claimed, and attacked her, scratching her hands and face tearing her clothes. Her screams brought a clerk from Renberg's store to her assistance and the Negro fled. He was captured and identified this morning both by the girl and clerk, police say. Rowland denied that he tried to harm the girl, but admitted he put his hand on her arm in the elevator when she was alone. Tenants of the Drexel building said the girl is an orphan who works as an elevator operator to pay her way through business college.

HERMAN. There they go telling lies. According to Dick, that is not the way it happened.

DADDY. Yea, but don't you see this is how them papers get white folks all riled up!

MARGARET. That's why I like to see what the papers is doing to manipulate and propagandize the white folk.

DADDY. Propagandize? Look at her Mama. Using words that we don't even know about. Girl, where did you learn a word like propagandize?

MARGARET. Booker T.

DADDY. Well I be damned. Girl it's time for you to go to another level.

MARGARET. Daddy there is more. The editorial says, "To Lynch Negro Tonight."

DADDY. Oh, so they saying they going to lynch the Negro tonight. See that's why we had to go down there. Smitherman, Wilson, the Mann Brothers, me, all of us were right. We have got to take a stand and stop them peckerwoods from misusing us.

(**ISAIAH** *bursts in the front door. He is very excited, and he notices* **DADDY** *sitting at the dining room table).*

ISAIAH. Daddy!

DADDY. Boy! Remind me to give you an ass whooping! What's going on out there now?

ISAIAH. Daddy I-

DADDY. I know. Your Mama told me she sent you out there this time, but the first time you didn't do what I told you to do, so even though you about to tell us what's going on, when this thing is over, I got something for you. Now tell me what is going on!

ISAIAH. The white folks are killing Negroes. They even trying to pass for colored by putting on make-up and trying to look black. John Johnson say he heard them saying they was going to get airplanes and start bombing Little Africa.

DADDY. Little Africa?

MARGARET. Yea Daddy. That's what they call Greenwood. The reason they call it that is because Negroes are successful with their businesses and everything.

ISAIAH. When I was running down the tracks there were a lot of Negroes fleeing north. Cecil Jenkins said he was trying to make it to that white man Dick Barton on the count that he would pawn stuff to black folks. Cecil felt like Mr. Barton might help him get away 'cause he's real nice to coloreds.

MAMA. Help him from getting killed?

ISAIAH. Yes ma'am. They say there is a whole lot of white folks that's just killing Negroes for no reason. John say we all need to be careful.

DADDY. Never mind tell me later. Right now, Herman, take Isaiah with you and go get them rifles out the bushes! Hurry!

HERMAN. Come on!

(HERMAN and ISAIAH exit out the kitchen.)

LEIGH. Mama. I couldn't even get down to Greenwood. All I heard shooting and the smell of smoke everywhere. It seems like they burning up the place. People was passing me saying get off Greenwood. So, I turned around and ran back home.

MARGARET. I heard that too. I saw Mrs. Minter and her sister, and she was wailing about her husband being killed down at the courthouse. They say it was a big fight that broke out and lot of Negroes and white folks got killed. Daddy I am glad you and Herman are okay. What happened?

DADDY. Thelma, you and Delma go to your sister's bedroom and tell them what happened. Mama help me over to that couch over there, so I can lay down. Y'all go to bed and get some rest. I'll wait for Isaiah and Herman.

(THELMA starts telling MARGARET and LEIGH what happened as MAMA helps DADDY to the couch. After a long pause DADDY speaks.)

DADDY. Mattie. I killed three white men tonight. It just seems so senseless. But with each one of them I could see the hate in their eyes. They won't get to come back home to their families like me. If they had wives, they won't get to caress them one last time.

MAMA. That's why I'm scared Alex. I just don't know what I would do if you wasn't here with this family. I love you and your children love you. Could you imagine what little Robert or sweet Mildred would be like without your loving care?

DADDY. Yes. I don't want to think about that. Help me sit up.

(**MAMA** *helps him sit up*).

MAMA. Our family is all we got Alex. I want to be able to see them grow up and raise their own families and have grandchildren.

DADDY. Yes, those oldest two boys and two girls is turning out to be some pretty good young men and women.

MAMA. Yes. But you done gave them a strong foundation. You taught them how to love and care for each other. You taught them that if they wanted something they would have to work hard for it.

DADDY. You ain't been no slouch either now. You the one that's been the businesswoman. You always trying to figure out how to make a dollar out of fifteen cents.

(**DADDY** *puts his arms around* **MAMA'S** *shoulders and squeezes her affectionately*).

MAMA. You remember when we first met?

DADDY. Now you know, you are not going to let me forget it.

MAMA. No, I want to know if you really remember. Or maybe you're trying to get me to tell you.

DADDY. I remember it like it was yesterday. You and your well-to-do family in Haskell. It was at the Morris Chapel picnic. And you had on that pretty yellow dress.

MAMA. Alex, you do remember.

DADDY. Mattie. I told you! I remember it like it was yesterday. Now, let me ask you. Do you remember the first thing I said to you?

MAMA. How can I forget? I don't know your name, but I hope you marry me someday.

DADDY. So, you do remember?

MAMA. Of course, I do. And here we are eight kids later.

(**MAMA** *starts crying.*)

DADDY. What's wrong baby? Aren't you happy?

MAMA. Remember, how long we held it from the children that you killed a white man. Now you done killed three more of them. You know they're coming after you. I am sure somebody saw you and Herman with the rest of them colored men.

DADDY. Now you know they all say we look alike. They ain't gon' know.

MAMA. That's not funny.

DADDY. Okay, Mattie Okay. We got a little time to think about it. They killed us too. It was a battle that we fought and sooner or later, people will just forget about it. White folks and colored folks died so we move on and forget about it.

MAMA. Do you think we will have to move away from Tulsa?

DADDY. Why are we gon' to do that?

MAMA. I just got a bad feeling Alex. We need to be safe.

DADDY. Mattie, stop worrying. We are safe. Herman is making it pretty good as a barber. Men folks gon' always need a haircut. Isaiah really likes fixing shoes and he's getting some good training to take over the shop one day. Now Leigh is really designing and sewing some nice clothes. You have showed her everything she needs to know. And, that Margaret is sharp! She don't like doing housework and that is gon' push here enough to pay her own way through college. She gon' be happy in a few months when we give her that little nest egg we been saving to let her get started at Langston University. And Thelma is going to be that nurse if she sticks to it. And that Delma is a good athlete. And ain't no telling what Robert is gon' do, and little Mildred loves to sing. We got to do all we can to make sure that they live long lives, but with dignity.

MAMA. I know Alex. I just worry sometime though. I just want so much for our children. And I have never regretted the day we got married.

DADDY. And, I don't regret the first day I met you when I said,

DADDY AND MAMA. I don't know your name, but I hope you marry me someday

(They both laugh as the lights fade.)

End of Scene Two

Scene Three

(June 1, 1921 - 12:30 a.m. **DADDY** *and* **MAMA** *are now sleep on the sofa cuddled up together.* **HERMAN** *and* **ISAIAH** *burst through the back door and run into the living room.* **DADDY** *and* **MAMA** *are startled and wake up quickly.)*

HERMAN. Daddy! It's crazy out there. These white folks have gone crazy!

ISAIAH. It's gone Daddy! It's gone!

DADDY. Boy what are you talking about! What's gone!

ISAIAH. The shoe shop and the seamstress shop. All gone. Burned down.

DADDY. What?! What the hell you mean son?!

HERMAN. The white folks are burning down Greenwood Daddy! Two blocks of Greenwood on one side is gone and the family businesses are gone!

DADDY. Those damn peckerwoods! Did you get the guns?!

HERMAN. We got them, but we ain't got no more ammunition for the shotgun.

ISAIAH. Look in the cabinet again in the kitchen.

HERMAN. I looked earlier. All we got left are bullets for the pistol.

DADDY. What did those white folks do?! What did they do?!

MAMA. Be careful Daddy! You are going to wake up the children.

DADDY. This is a damn shame! This is a damn shame!

ISAIAH. Daddy, the white folks are not only burning Greenwood, but they are killing Negroes for no reason.

DADDY. What are you talking about son? Them white folks ain't that crazy.

HERMAN. We ran into Jesse Guess and he said that they killed Dr. A.C. Jackson, the surgeon, and he had his hands up. He says it's a big mob of white folks just shooting, killing and burning. He said he heard the police were with the mob too.

*(***LEIGH, MARGARET, DELMA, THELMA, ROBERT*** *and* **MILDRED** *enter the room.)*

55

DADDY. This is crazy! These peckerwoods are sick!

MAMA. Oh Lord! What are we going to do? What are we going to do?

HERMAN. Daddy when me and Isaiah got the guns, we had to hide in the bushes cause a white mob had Willie and Maggie's Smith son Bo and his pregnant wife-

LEIGH. Mary?

ISAIAH. That's her. They strung Willie up to a tree and lynched him. Then they strung Mary up and lynched her too!

LEIGH. Jesus no!

ISAIAH. I can't tell the rest. Herman, you tell them.

HERMAN. Well, they, they-

DADDY. Spit it out boy! Spit it out!

HERMAN. They cut her stomach open and the baby came out crying! Then one of them said, "Shut that boy up!" And they threw the baby on the to the ground and stomped it dead.

(The small children start crying. **THELMA** *and* **DELMA** *are in shock.* **LEIGH** *and* **MARGARET** *is frightened.* **HERMAN** *is pacing, and* **ISAIAH** *is angry.)*

DADDY. BE QUIET! LISTEN. Listen.

(Everyone gets very quiet, except for **ROBERT** *who is whimpering.* **MILDRED** *is holding tight to* **THELMA'S** *skirt. The distant sound of a large crowd, people screaming, and gunshots are heard in the distance.* **HERMAN** *looks outside the dining room window.)*

HERMAN. *(whispering)* It's a whole crowd of white folks coming down street. They're shooting people as they run. Negroes is falling like flies. Some of them are next door and here come-

(The gunshots get louder, and the crowd noise get louder as the lights black out quickly.)

End of Scene 3

Scene 4

(June 1, 1921 – 1:30 a.m. The stage is completely dark and empty. This part of the scene is done with pre-recorded sound. The sound should be loud throughout. There is no music throughout the scene. There is a lot of commotion in the dark. The following dialogue is heard through the many gunshots, fighting, scuffling, screams, crying, moaning, etc.

DADDY. PECKERWOODS!

MAMA. NO! NO! NO! NO!

HERMAN. GET HIM ISAIAH!

ISAIAH. YOU AIN'T NOBODY

LEIGH. STOP! STOP! DON'T TOUCH ME! DON'T TOUCH ME!

THELMA. AAAAAAAAAAAAAA AAAAAA! RUN MILDRED RUN!

ROBERT. LEAVE MY BROTHER ALONE! LEAVE MY BROTHER ALONE!

DELMA. WATCH OUT DADDY! GET HIM HERMAN! TAKE THIS PECKERWOOD!

WHITE MAN #1. SHOOT 'EM ALL!

WHITE MAN #2. KILL 'EM! UPPITY NIGGERS!

THELMA. LEAVE MY MAMA ALONE!

WHITE MAN #3. WHO YOU CALLING A PECKERWOOD NIGGER?!

MARGARET. LEEEIIIGGGGHHHHHHH!!!!

WHITE MAN #4. NIGGERS DON'T DESERVE TO LIVE

WHITE MAN#5. WATCH YOURSELF GAL! IT'S OVER FOR YOU!

WHITE MAN# 3. UPPITY NIGGERS!!

MARGARET. PLEASE DON'T KILL ME! PLEASE DON'T KILL ME!

WHITE MAN #5. YOU DEAD NOW GIRLIE! YIIIIHHHAAAAAY!

(The last gunshot is heard.)

WHITE MAN # 1. ARE THEY ALL DEAD?!

WHITE MAN #2. WE GOT 'EM ALL.

WHITE MAN #3. KILLED EVERY ONE OF THEM BASTARDS!

WHITE MAN #1. LOOKS LIKE THEY GOT LITTLE TATE AND COUSIN LUTHER!

WHITE MAN #3. DAMN! YOU BOYS WATCH YOURSELF! WE CAN'T AFFORD TO LOSE NO MORE OF YOU.

WHITE MAN #1. LET'S GO TO THE NEXT HOUSE!

WHITE MAN #2. LET'S GO BOYS REMEMBER EVERY ONE OF THEM NIGGERS DIES!

*(The lights fade up slowly. Everyone is lying still. The room is very quiet. Everyone is dead. **DADDY** is lying on the floor in front of the sofa with his face down. **MAMA** is lying next to **DADDY** near the sofa. **MARGARET** is downstage right near the kitchen table. **HERMAN** is near **MARGARET** on the floor. **LEIGH** is draped over the sofa. **ISAIAH** is near the front door on the floor. **ROBERT** is upstage of the dining room table. **DELMA** is downstage from **DADDY** and **MAMA**. **WHITE MAN # 4** downstage right of **MARGARET** on the floor. **ISAIAH** is on the slightly downstage left side near the door. **WHITE MAN #5** on the floor near **ISAIAH**. **THELMA** is center stage. After a short while, **MILDRED** emerges from the downstage right bedroom. She walks over to **MARGARET** and shakes her. **MARGARET** does not respond. She goes to **WHITE MAN #4** and steps away from him quickly. She slowly walks to **HERMAN** and kneels. She shakes **HERMAN'S** shoulder and gets blood on her hands. She stands and goes upstage to **ROBERT**. She shakes **ROBERT** and he does not move. She slowly walks over to **LEIGH** on the couch. She stares at **LEIGH**. She walks between **DADDY** and **MAMA** and gets on her knees and shakes both of their shoulders as she whimpers. She shakes **DELMA** and he does not respond. She rises and walks slowly to **ISAIAH** downstage left. She shakes his feet. She rises and stands over **THELMA** and stares at her lifeless body. She looks towards the sky and sings very slowly)*

MILDRED. *(singing)*
Jesus loves me this I know
For the bible tells me so
Little ones to him belong
They are weak, but he is strong
Yes, Jesus loves me
Yes, Jesus loves me
Yes, Jesus loves me
The bible tells me so

*(**MILDRED** looks straight ahead at the audience as the pinpoint light on her face fades).*

End of Scene Four

Scene Five

(The curtain call is a tableau of the family. It should resemble a family portrait. Everyone is in a frozen position. The lighting should make everyone in the portrait appear to be in black and white. No members of the family should smile. **DADDY** *and* **MAMA** *should be seated in chairs from the dining room in the middle.* **MILDRED** *and* **ROBERT** *should be seated on the floor in front of* **MAMA** *and* **DADDY***. In the back row and standing behind* **MAMA** *and* **DADDY** *should be* **ISAIAH**, **DELMA**, **THELMA**, **MARGARET**, **LEIGH**, *and* **HERMAN**.

(The lights fade)

End of Scene Five

END OF PLAY

Inspired by God

STORY TWO

GREENWOOD

CHARACTERS

BIG MAMA – 60-70-year-old woman that is wise for her years and lives with her daughter.

LEROY – 20-year-old grandson of Big Mama who is quick-tempered.

MOE – 17-year-old brother of Leroy who is physically built.

JAMES – 40-year-old man trying to take care of his family.

LUVENIA – 35-year-old wife of James strong willed and tough.

BUD – 10-year-old son of James and Luvenia

PAPA – 60-70 year educated businessman and investor

TRESSIE – 25-year-old daughter of Papa who is homely and clean

RUTH – 19-year-old daughter of Papa who uses her looks to tame men.

JEAN – 40-year-old daughter of Big Mama who is religious.

MILDRED – 10-year-old orphan girl

MATTHEW – 30- year-old man who is strong and tough.

Setting

The early summer of 1921 in Tulsa, Oklahoma

Act 1

Scene 1

A campground in Mohawk park in the early morning about 1:00 a.m. on June 1, 1921.

Scene 2

A campground in Mohawk park in the early morning about 5:45 a.m. on June 1, 1921.

Scene 3

A shed near Mohawk park in the early morning about 7:00 a.m. on June 1, 1921.

Scene 4

A clearing in Mohawk park in the morning about 8:00 a.m. on June 1, 1921.

Scene 5

An area in Mohawk park in the morning about 8:30 a.m. on June 1, 1921.

Scene 6

A shed near Mohawk park in the morning about 9:00 a.m. on June 1, 1921.

Scene 7

An area in Mohawk park in the morning about 10:00 a.m. on June 1, 1921

Scene 8

A campground in Mohawk park in the early afternoon about 12:00 noon on June 1, 1921

Act 2

Scene 1

McNulty Park in the afternoon about 3:00 p.m. on June 1, 1921.

Scene 2

Convention Hall in the afternoon about 4:00 p.m. on June 1, 1921

Scene 3

McNulty Park in the afternoon about 5:00 p.m. on June 1, 1921

Scene 4

Convention Hall in the evening about 6:00 p.m. on June 1, 1921

Scene 5

The ruins of homes in the Greenwood District in the evening about 7:00 p.m. on June 1, 1921

Scene 6

Curtain Call

ACT I

Scene One

(It is early morning about 1:00 a.m. on June 1, 1921.)

(There is an open area downstage center. A tree stump and a few rocks are available for sitting. There are about seven small rocks circled together as if there was a campfire. There are a few small branches and logs gathered together for possible storage for another fire. **LEROY** *enters. He looks around and surveys the area.)*

LEROY. Come on Moe. This is that spot we were at the last time we were fishing with Daddy. I told you we were close to it. And, it wasn't too far from the road. I bet she can rest here on this rock.

*(***MOE** *enters with* **BIG MAMA** *who walks pretty good although she has a cane.).*

BIG MAMA. Boy, I done told you I can walk. I ain't that damn old. I've been getting around for the past 60 years and I can still get around now. I wished we wouldn't have left as early as we did. I'd like to be there to shoot some of them damn crackers myself. Your Daddy talking about making us get in that old truck and come north. How we know the damn thing would stop on us and we'd have to walk the rest of the way to Lynn Lane.

MOE. We just had a flat Big Mama. We will get it fixed in the morning. You won't have to walk no more. Daddy knows how to fix it. And if he don't, we'll take it to Mr. Grayson's shop.

BIG MAMA. I can't understand your Daddy. Never have understood him. How he gon' tell us to go North just in case there's some trouble, knowing his wife is on the south side of town taking care of white folk's children. She don't know where we at or what the hell he's doing.

LEROY. Big Mama, he said that he is gon' call her from the Tulsa Star and let her know.

MOE. Plus, he says he gon' go by the restaurant on Greenwood and tell Georgia and Grace, so they can tell her where we're at, if she comes home. She said that she might have to stay in the maid quarters tonight, 'cause Ms. Agnes wanted her to do some extra ironing. Plus, before she come home, you know she always stop by the family restaurant and help Daddy, Georgia and Grace close up the place. Big Mama, I think Daddy wanted us to go ahead, just to be on the safe side.

BIG MAMA. That's why I am not scared to tell my son-in-law, your Daddy, and your Mama's husband, that he is stupid!

LEROY. Maybe you just need to get some rest Big Mama. That was a long walk. I got these blankets. Do you want some water? I brought that too.

BIG MAMA. No. This rock right here will do me some good. Is that smoke I smell?

MOE. Yes. I smelled it about a half hour ago. It seems like it's getting worse. I hope ain't nobody's house burned down or nothing.

BIG MAMA. Got me out here in these damn woods at 1:00 in the morning. This don't make no sense. I needs my beauty rest.

LEROY. I think this is a good place for us to bed down tonight Big Mama. This a nice good spot 'cause we been out this way with Daddy fishing. We should be all right here until in the morning.

BIG MAMA. Leroy! Damn. I need you to run back to that car and get my purse. I forgot my purse in the car and I need me a smoke.

LEROY. Yes ma'am

*(**LEROY** runs off stage quickly.)*

BIG MAMA. And hurry boy!

MOE. Big Mama, do you think Daddy and the rest of them Negro men gon' stop them white folks from lynching Dick Rowland?

BIG MAMA. Can a cat swim?

MOE. *(confused)* I ain't never seen a cat swim Big Mama.

BIG MAMA. Then you just answered your question.

MOE. What do you mean Big Mama?

BIG MAMA. Moe, you are starting to act just like your Daddy. I think you took more to him and his side of the family instead of your Mama's side.

MOE. Huh?

BIG MAMA. Damn boy! Naw! If them crackers want to lynch that boy then they gon' lynch him. Them Negroes can't stop them white folks from lynching Dick Rowland. That boy is just as good as gone!

MOE. Daddy say that Negroes got to stand for something Big Mama. He says all we do is let the white man treat us any kind of way. He says if we keep doing that, we are not men. He says we just might as well have stayed slaves. He said if we don't stand up, we just some stupid white folks Negroes that don't have a mind of our own.

BIG MAMA. Your Daddy got spirit. I give him that much! But, his spirit is lacking common sense. He need to take care of his own business before he start messing around in other folk's business.

(BIG MAMA reaches in her dress pocket and pulls out a pipe and tobacco.)

BIG MAMA. Lord have mercy. Here is my pipe and tobacco. Well, I still need my purse. Give me that blanket and I'm gon' lay down and get me some rest, I'm tired.

(LEROY runs in quickly and is out of breath. He gives her the purse.)

LEROY. Here you go Big Mama.

BIG MAMA. Thanks baby. I guess the both of you should lay down and go to sleep. Hopefully, we will be back home tomorrow.

(LEROY and MOE take a blanket and lay down and go to sleep as the lights fade.)

End of Scene One

Scene Two

June 1, 1921 at 5:45 a.m. **BIG MAMA**, **LEROY** *and* **MOE** *are sleep.* **BIG MAMA** *holds a pistol in her hand as she sleeps.* **LEROY** *and* **MOE** *are both snoring. A loud whistle or horn is heard from a distance. It sounds like a train. It wakes* **BIG MAMA**, **LEROY** *and* **MOE** *up as they rise quickly.)*

BIG MAMA. What the hell is that?

(Sounds of an airplane flying low are heard. In the distance machine gun fire is heard. A sound of another airplane flying low is heard. **BIG MAMA** *points her gun around and looks for possible intruders.)*

LEROY. Sounds like a plane. Those planes sure are low.

MOE. What kind of whistle is that? It sounds like a train.

(In the distance a bomb is heard.)

BIG MAMA. Ain't no telling. But, it sounds like them crackers is up to something.

MOE. Big Mama, what do we need to do?

BIG MAMA. First, we got to find out what the hell is going on. Now, both of you is old enough to take care of yourselves. As long as I got old Roscoe here, I can take care of myself. Y'all go back to town and see what's going on. But, be careful. If you run into some trouble, stay hidden and quiet until you see what them white folks is up to. Whatever you do, stay together. Don't get separated. You need to both protect each other.

LEROY. Big Mama, are you sure you will be okay.

BIG MAMA. Boy, didn't I tell you I had Roscoe. Now git!

*(***LEROY** *and* **MOE** *run off stage.)*

BIG MAMA. Well, I'll be damned!

(The lights fade to black.)

End of Scene Two

Scene Three

(June 1, 1921 at 7:00 a.m. There is a small shed sitting downstage right. It has tools, supplies, and various paraphernalia inside. **JAMES** *enters the door upstage center of the shed and looks in. He gazes around the shed and cleans up an area on the floor. He is sweating very hard and his shirt is torn and wet. There is blood coming from his arm and he winces in pain. He walks back out of the door and motions for someone to come in.* **LUVENIA** *and young* **BUD** *slowly walk in the shed.* **LUVENIA** *is dressed in a night gown.* **BUD** *is dressed in some long johns and limping. There is blood on the top and bottom of his left foot.* **JAMES** *motions for* **BUD** *to sit near the wall and* **LUVENIA** *sits near* **BUD**.*)

JAMES. We should be able to rest here awhile. This ole' shed is out here in the woods a ways and I remembers my daddy built it near that old dug well. We lived out here in a tepee Daddy got from the Creek Indians before we moved near Greenwood. We should be safe here for a while.

LUVENIA. James are you sure?

JAMES. Yes Luvenia, I'm sure.

BUD. Mama I cut my foot running through them rocks on the railroad tracks.

LUVENIA. Here baby, let me look at it. Whoo wee, you got a big gash on that foot of yours.

BUD. Yes'm, it hurts real bad.

JAMES. You just gon' have to let it hurt for a while son. It might be a while before we can doctor it up. I'll try to get us some water out of that well in a few minutes.

LUVENIA. James, I thought you said didn't nobody know about this place.

JAMES. I'm telling you Daddy had always planned to leave it for us to have. We way out north past Apache and almost to 36th St. North. Mohawk ain't too far from here
. Ain't no white folks coming out here.

BUD. Daddy we run a long ways. I didn't think we would ever stop running.

JAMES. A little exercise will do you some good son. We just grateful that through all of that running, we didn't get caught.

BUD. Daddy! How many miles we run.

LUVENIA. Hush up now Bud. You ask your Daddy too many questions.

BUD. I was just asking.

LUVENIA. Like I said hush up now. Your Daddy got to think about what we gon' do now.

BUD. *(yawning)* I'm tired Mama. I am so sleepy! All I's remember is this loud whistle like a train waking me up. Then I heard all of these gun shots going pow, pow, pow, pow, pow, pow, pow, pow. But Mama, can I ask Daddy one more question?

JAMES. Go ahead son. What is your question?

BUD. Daddy I know we was running fast. I could see the bullets hitting the dirt. I almost got hit by something that exploded and the dirt hit my leg and I fell. I'm glad you grabbed me by my britches and told me to keep running.

JAMES. Boy, I thought you had a question?

BUD. Yes sir.

JAMES. Then ask the question son.

BUD. Why them white men want to kill us Daddy? We ain't done nothing to nobody. You just woke me up and told me to run. I didn't even have time to put my shoes on. Then them white folks started shooting up Mr. McCondichie's house next door and shooting people. I saw Joe Simpson's daddy running with us and he fell dead. Why them white folks want to kill us Daddy? Why? We ain't done nothing.

JAMES. Well son, it's a long story and it will take too long to tell it to you right now. You get some rest. Hand me that bucket over there.

(**BUD** hands **JAMES** the bucket.)

BUD. *(yawns)* Okay Daddy. Here you go.

LUVENIA. Come here baby. Lay your head on Mama's lap.

(**LUVENIA** rubs **BUD'S** head as she sings him a lullaby. A very sleepy **BUD** closes his eyes as she sings. **JAMES** stares into space.)

LUVENIA. *(singing)*
Go to sleep
Go to sleep
Go to sleep little baby
When you wake
When you wake
You'll find two pretty white horses.
Bah Bah black sheep

Where is your lamb?
Way over in the pasture.
The buzzards and the flies
Keep picking at his eyes.
Poor little thing cried, mama.

(**BUD** *starts snoring.* **JAMES** *looks at* **BUD** *and notices he is already sleep.*)

JAMES. The boy must have been really tired.

LUVENIA. Ain't every day you get woke out the middle of your sleep and have to run for your life. How many miles we run?

JAMES. Oh, about five. Luvenia they had them airplanes and they was dropping bombs on us.

LUVENIA. Bombs and shooting bullets. They must want us dead bad.

JAMES. Yes. But folks were talking about Dick Rowland and that white girl all day yesterday. And when them Negroes like Goodwin, Stradford, and Smitherman went down to that courthouse to stop Rowland from getting lynched, them white folks must have lost their minds.

LUVENIA. James we just up and left. What about our house? We done almost got it paid off where we own it. I hope it's still there when we get back, 'cause it's what we've been working so hard for the last ten years. Them planes was flying real low and one of them bombs hit Lula Jones' house and it just blew up.

JAMES. It will be there baby. It will be there.

LUVENIA. I still see Norma Lee in my mind James. It's just like they just gunned her down. She run out of the house and only had on her bra and panties and this lil' boy couldn't been no more than 10 or 12 just shot her four times. James, it was so horrible. Norma Lee? She was always so sweet.

JAMES. Don't think about it baby. Just thank the good Lord that you are still here.

LUVENIA. She was my cousin James. And when we hid in the bushes I looked back and saw Ennis on fire. I wanted to come out of them bushes from where we were hiding to put him out, but I was so scared, it wasn't nothing I could do. And I know Bud is going to remember it too. They had already shot Ennis to death. Why did they have to burn him too? And when Bud started whimpering, I just knew they would hear us. I put my hand over his mouth so hard, he 'bout bit my hand.

JAMES. I know Luvenia. I saw it too. But God saw fit for us to make it this far. It was an angel of God that guided us. Hopefully, this thing will be over soon, and we can get

71

back home. I'm going to go out here and get some water out of that well. You rest a minute and I will be right back.

LUVENIA. James.

JAMES. Yes, baby.

LUVENIA. You be careful here.

> (**JAMES** *walks out of the door.* **LUVENIA** *sits next to* **BUD** *as the lights fade to black.*)

End of Scene Three

Scene 4

(June 1, 1921 at 8:00 a.m. **PAPA** *is sitting alone on a tree stump upstage left. He looks to his left as* **TRESSIE** *and* **RUTH** *enter.* **TRESSIE** *is homely looking.* **RUTH** *is light-skinned and considered by many to be a pretty girl.* **RUTH** *is dressed in a hot red dress. They look distraught, tired and weary.)*

PAPA. I guess they ain't got too many outhouses out here in these parts. I think we are in Mohawk.

TRESSIE. I guess they ain't Papa. But me and Ruth had to go. We found a good bush over yonder and that made it a little easy.

RUTH. Girl these woods are for the birds. Ain't no slop jar or nothing. This country living ain't for me.

*(***RUTH** *takes a mirror out of her purse along with some red lipstick. She starts to put the lipstick on her lips as she looks at herself in the mirror.)*

TRESSIE. Okay Miss Prissy. You might have to come off your high horse for a while.

RUTH. Girl, I know I was not gon' be able to walk way out here. Wherever we are. When y'all start saying we had to go before trouble got started, I already knew I was gon' have to find me a ride. We left too early in the morning. When I heard that horn sound and them guns start firing, I knew something was wrong. Good thing Pawpaw saw that white man who let us ride in the back of his wagon. I think I messed up my stockings when we had to lay down and hide to keep them white folks from seeing us before we got to Pine.

TRESSIE. Yes, they had Pine and Greenwood blocked off. It looked like they wouldn't let no colored folks through.

PAPA. If it wouldn't have been for that old white friend of mine Mr. Bell, we'd all probably been dead by now. When we had to hide at that check point they set up, I thought we was gon' get caught for sho'.

RUTH. Caught? But we ain't done nothing. I don't know what the fuss is about. When I left the Choc joint they was talking about Dick Rowland and that white girl, but I don't know who they're kidding. I saw both of them at the joint the other night. They were dancing and kissing. They should have gone to the Royal or Red Wing hotel the way they were carrying on. And tonight, humph, Bubba was getting ready to give me some of his corn whiskey when some boys came in and said we better leave cause of the trouble down on deep Greenwood. I appreciate Bubba, 'cause he was nice enough to walk me home.

TRESSIE. Girl, you just don't pay no attention to nobody except yourself, do you? You best be glad you got home.

RUTH. I got home about eleven. I needed my beauty rest. I still got on the dress I had on last night. I guess I passed out from Bubba's corn whiskey we drank on the way home. I was good until you come waking me up about 4:30 talking about we had to go. Daddy. Who was that white man?

PAPA. Mr. Bell is good white folks. In this case, he got a chance to return the favor. See, years ago, I saved his life.

TRESSIE. Saved his life?

PAPA. Yes'm. Oh, reckon it was about 30 years ago and I was working for Mr. Bell on his place plowing the fields. He was coming down the road on his horse. Well the horse got spooked or something and reared up and threw Mr. Bell. Well, the horse took off running. When he fell off the horse Mr. Bell was sitting up, but he wasn't moving. So, I high tailed it over there where he was sitting. When I got close I saw what he was looking at. It was two rattle snakes rolled up around each other and it looked like they was mating. And they was about 6 inches from his boots. So, I asked Mr. Bell, I say, Mr. Bell are you hurt. He said, "No sir." I said, okay. I said, I'm gon' distract them and when I do, you high tail it out of there as fast as you can. He said, "Don't worry." So, I picked up a couple of rocks. I eased myself to the right of Mr. Bell and I was standing about ten feet away from him and those snakes. I chunked that rock and hit one of them snakes right on the head and Mr. Bell took out like a jackrabbit running from a dog. One of the snakes ran off, but I killed one, and me and Mr. Bell laughed about that for years.

TRESSIE. That's something Papa. I didn't know you used to work for Mr. Bell. He seemed to always act like he didn't like us.

PAPA. Well, we fell out about ten years ago. Mr. Bell thought I was trying to cheat him out of his money and he told me not to come back again.

TRESSIE. Pawpaw he saw us walking. He knew you was moving slow with your cane. Was that why he stopped his horse to give us a ride?

PAPA. You saw him didn't you.

RUTH. I saw him look at you for a long time and you looked back at him. Then he says, get in. I sure was glad, 'cause I was starting to sweat. I can't be sweating. It don't look good for a pretty girl like me. We got in and started riding, and I was fine until he told us to hide under them blankets.

TRESSIE. You didn't see all them colored folks down there trying to get through. I could hear folks talking when we were under the blankets. Girl I know you heard them white men telling folks to get back, get back. Then there was a whole lot more shooting and folks started screaming and hollering. Then, after we stopped for a while, you could hear the white men say, let the white man through, let the white man through.

RUTH. I heard 'em. I heard 'em. Now that was kind of scary!

TRESSIE. He helped us get out of there.

RUTH. But, did he have to drop us off in the woods? Girl, it's all kind of creatures out here.

TRESSIE. When we got out Pawpaw, you and him looked at each other again. Y'all looked at each other for a long spell and didn't neither one of you say a word. Then he just drove off.

PAPA. Ah naw, baby. We talked. We talked. It was all in the mind. All in the mind. We need to keep moving. I know there is a creek around here somewhere. We need to find us some water.

(*PAPA walks off stage as* **TRESSIE** *and* **RUTH** *follow him.*)

RUTH. Creek? Creek water? Pawpaw you don't know somebody with a farm house or something that's got a well somewhere?

(*They exit stage left as the lights fade.*)

End of Scene Four

Scene 5

*(June 1, 1921 at 8:30 a.m. The lights come up center stage on **JEAN** and **MILDRED**. **MILDRED** is sitting on the grass crying.)*

JEAN. Come on baby, I know, I know. You got to stop crying.

*(**MILDRED** continues to cry and whimper.)*

MILDRED. *(crying)* They de-de-de DEEEAAADDDDDD!

*(**JEAN** grabs **MILDRED** and holds her tight and starts rocking her back and forth.)*

JEAN. It's okay baby. It's okay. It's gon' be all right. Jean is gon' to take care of you now. You got Jean baby, you got Jean. There's a scripture in the bible. It is Romans 8:28 and it says, "All things come together for the good, for them that love God." God done put Jean here to help you baby. Jean is gon' help you.

MILDRED. I'm scared!

JEAN. I know baby. I know. We all scared! We all scared!

MILDRED. Them white men did it! Them white men did it!

JEAN. You safe with Jean, baby. You safe with Jean.

*(**JEAN** here's a noise offstage. She squeezes **MILDRED** tight.)*

JEAN. Who's there?

MATTHEW. Sorry. I didn't mean to scare you.

JEAN. Show yourself!

*(**MATTHEW** emerges out of the bushes.)*

MATTHEW. Sorry. I just been running. I ran up in these bushes and I saw you and your little girl. I didn't mean to scare you.

JEAN. It's okay. I guess we all running. And, so you know, she ain't my little girl. We both strays. I guess if you by yourself, you must be a stray to huh? Me and this one just done became attached. I don't even know her name. Baby, tell Jean your name.

MILDRED. Mildred.

MATTHEW. That's a beautiful name. Who give you that name?

MILDRED. *(crying)* Mam-

*(**MILDRED** starts crying again very loud.)*

JEAN. Hush now! It's all right. Jean here now. Jean here.

MATTHEW. I'm sorry. She must of-

*(**JEAN** puts her finger to her mouth to tell **MATTHEW** to be quiet. **MILDRED** continues to whimper as **JEAN** rocks her. **MILDRED** puts her thumb in her mouth. **MATTHEW** walks away as **JEAN** continues to rock **MILDRED**.)*

JEAN. (softly) Jean is here Mildred. God got Jean here. It's gon' be all right. Jean is here. God got Jean here.

*(**MILDRED** slowly goes to sleep. **JEAN** lays her head on the ground and slowly stands. She walks over to **MATTHEW** and he turns around to **JEAN**.)*

JEAN. What's your name?

MATTHEW. Matthew.

JEAN. Who your people?

MATTHEW. Ain't got none here. Just came in from Snake Creek a couple of months ago. Folks down there say, go north to Tulsa. In Snake Creek, they say they got a place down there called Greenwood and colored folks is living like kings and queens. So, me and my brother decided to head this way.

JEAN. I don't know no folks from Snake Creek. If all you got is you and your brother, and the rest of your kin is in Snake Creek, then what's your last name?

MATTHEW. Malone. Matthew Malone.

JEAN. Where's your brother?

*(**MATTHEW** puts his fist over his mouth and tries to hold back the tears. He walks away from **JEAN** and tries to gather himself.)*

JEAN. I'm sorry.

MATTHEW. He died in my arms. We were down there on Greenwood when this white mob came out of nowhere. We were coming out Vadel's pool hall and they just started shooting. We ran back in the pool hall and out the back door to the alley. We kept running, but they kept shooting. Roy got hit in the shoulder and we kept running. We hit the tracks and ran down the other side. Roy was running too, and it seemed like he was holding on, until he fell. I stopped to check on him and drug him to the bushes. When, I got him to where we could not be seen, I saw some white boys still running down the tracks. Roy was in worse shape than I thought cause blood was coming from his stomach. He had been shot two maybe three times. He say, "Little Brother, I'm hurt real bad. Say, "You going have to enjoy the promised land without me." Then he died right there. I'm sorry. All I could do was cry. Roy was a good fellow. He never hurt nobody. I just held on to him as all the shooting kept going on. After a while, I heard some more white folks coming. I knew they was white folks 'cause a how they says they wants to kill every Nigger they see. So, I took off running as far away from them as I could. Then, I heard this loud whistle and this machine gun was at the top of the hill and just shooting. I ran out of there and took for cover in the bushes, but it seems like it was getting closer to me where I was hiding. Then there was a airplane that was flying real close to the ground and they started dropping bombs. Buildings started burning up and folks started running. I started running too, but I didn't know which way to go. I just started following folks and running. I just been running until I saw you and the little girl. I don't know what I'm gon' do without Roy. I just-

(MATTHEW sits on the ground. He is silent for a moment as JEAN goes over to MILDRED who is sound asleep.)

JEAN. We all got our stories about this uprising don't we. It's sad. It's sad for me cause I don't know where my family is. I don't know if they are dead or alive. I hopes they are all alive and out here safe somewhere. Either way, God gon' lead me to them on his time. My husband is a good man. He takes care of all of us including my Mama. Well, Mama is an older woman and can be feisty at times. Mama don't take no mess and she help me raise my two girls and two boys. I got two girls one 22 and the other 20. I got two boys one 19 and the other one 17.

MATTHEW. You say you don't know if your family is dead or alive?

JEAN. No. I was in the maid quarters at Ms. Agnes' house and Mr. George wake me up at about 3:30 in the morning and tell me I better go home to my family 'cause there was gon' be some trouble. Well, he gave me a ride down to the Frisco tracks and I starts walking down Greenwood and I sees all the fires. I sees colored and white men lying dead on the streets. I starts running and when I gets to the house; ain't nobody home. I called for everybody and all I here is shooting going on and I come out side and see it's a whole lot of white men coming down the street. I saw them shoot Lula Jefferson in her front yard. So, I do what everybody else is doing and I start running. I ran as fast as I could, and I saw bullets bouncing off the street and hitting the trees and poles. I see this little girl crying her eyes out. She was just standing in the middle of the road crying. I grabbed her by the arm and told her to come with me. She kept crying, but she was running with me. We got out the road and ran into some bushes and trees. She stopped crying and grabbed my hand real hard. We ran into some sticker bushes and she started hollering about her feet. I picked her up and packed her until we got here. I didn't even know her name. I don't know her story. Poor thing must have gotten separated from her folks. Got to be from the way she been crying. Maybe after all this is over, God will help me find her people.

MATTHEW. Looks like that smoke is getting thicker. They must really be doing some burning. What you know about where we at right now?

JEAN. This here be a place they call Mohawk. We should be safe here in these woods. There should be a creek around here nearby to get some water. My husband and my boys come out here and go fishing. We should be all right until the dust settles.

(MATTHEW *sits down, and* JEAN *goes over and sit next to* MILDRED *as the lights fade.)*

End of Scene Five

Scene 6

(June 1, 1921 at 9:00 a.m. **JAMES** *walks in the door of the shed and startles*
LUVENIA*. She sighs in relief and notices it is him.* **JAMES** *sits down a bucket of water
and a mid-sized can on the floor of the shed. He kisses* **LUVENIA** *lightly as she gets up
to her knees. She checks on* **BUD** *who is still sound asleep. She rises to her feet and
looks at* **JAMES***.)*

JAMES. I got some fresh water out of that well. Ain't nothing like some fresh well water. I
helped myself to it and it is pretty good. Try some.

*(***LUVENIA** *takes a drink from the metal scoop in the bucket. She takes another
drink.)*

LUVENIA. This water ain't too bad.

JAMES. I picked some blackberries too. I just don't know. Luvenia, I saw a lot of smoke this
morning back towards town. Seems like the smoke is pretty thick. Almost look like it
is bad weather.

LUVENIA. You can see the smoke from here?

JAMES. Come on.

*(***LUVENIA** *looks at* **BUD***.)*

JAMES. He'll be all right. Come on.

*(***LUVENIA** *and* **JAMES** *leave the shed and come directly downstage of it.)*

LUVENIA. My Lord James. What is going on?

JAMES. I guess that boy must of gotten' lynched or them Negroes did something. I ain't never
seen nothing like this in all my born days.

LUVENIA. I was so glad when I saw you come home. I was so worried that you wouldn't make
it home from Mr. Luke and Miss. Sally's house. When you said get some clothes on
and get Bud up and let's go, I didn't know what to think. I knew you was supposed
to work late for Miss. Sally's birthday party, but I wasn't expecting you 'til next
evening.

JAMES. Yes, I was playing that piano and they was just a drinking and eating. Earl Gibson
came in and whispered something to Mr. Luke. Then, Mr. Luke told everybody to
leave. He told the help in the kitchen and all us colored folks to get out cause the
niggers in Niggertown is killing white men, women and children. Well, that was
enough for me, so, I took off. I caught a ride with Elwood Monroe and by the time

80

we got close to Greenwood, a white mob was breaking in the pawn shops downtown. I saw them loading guns and ammunition on a truck. Elwood backed up quick and we went around towards Cincinnati way and ran into some more white folks. Me and Elwood got out of the car and start running North. When we got to Standpipe Hill it was about fifty Negroes on top of the hill lined up shooting at white folks. Bullets started coming from everywhere. When we saw white folks shooting back at the Negroes we both took off west and ran around the hill. We just kept running. When we ran we saw white folks just dropping down dead. I could see that old Horace Peg Leg Taylor was knocking white folks off like it wasn't nothing. He had some young boys loading up three rifles at a time. As soon as he unloaded one rifle they would give him another. Them Negroes was holding them white folks down. If them white folks weren't dead, they were almost dead. By the time we got around the hill, I didn't know where Elwood was. All I could think of was getting home. I could see the white folks starting to push the Negroes off the hill 'cause it was so many white folks coming at once and the Negroes couldn't shoot them fast enough. I figured the best thing for me to do was run home, get you and Bud and keep running north. And when I got home that's when I told you and the boy we had to go. I don't know where Elwood is or if he even made it.

LUVENIA. What we gon' do now James? How are we gon' make it?

JAMES. Well, first off, you and Bud are safe here. Go ahead and eat them blackberries. If the boy wants some more, you can pick 'em, just make sure you get a stick and rattle the berry patch first. Them ole' snakes like them berries too. So, you be careful.

LUVENIA. What you gon' do James?

JAMES. Well, Luvenia I'mo head back. I got to see what is going on now. Maybe this whole thing done settled down.

LUVENIA. James, I'm scared.

JAMES. I'm scared too Luvenia, but we ain't got no choice right now. I should be back before this afternoon. If I ain't back before the sun starts to set, start heading to town. I will meet you at the house.

LUVENIA. But James, what if you ain't at the house.

JAMES. Meet me at the house Luvenia. Do you remember the way?

LUVENIA. Just go towards town until I get to Pine. Then go right. I got it.

(**JAMES** and **LUVENIA** embrace. They look at each other and **JAMES** walks off stage left as she watches him for a minute. She goes back into the shed as the lights fade to black.)

End of Scene Six

Scene 7

June 1, 1921 at 10:00 a.m. **JEAN** *and* **MILDRED** *are laying on the ground sleeping.* **MILDRED** *is playing with a stick and digging it into the ground.* **MATTHEW** *is sitting on the ground with his arms wrapped around his knees as* **JEAN** *slowly sits up.)*

MILDRED. *(singing)*
Jesus loves me this I know
For the bible tells me so
Little ones to him belong
They are weak, but he is strong.

*(***JEAN** *joins* **MILDRED** *singing the song.)*

JEAN AND MILDRED *(singing)*
Yes, Jesus loves me
Yes, Jesus loves me
Yes, Jesus loves me
The bible tells me so.

JEAN. That's a pretty song Mildred. Did you learn that song in church?

MILDRED. My sister taught it to me. I'm in the church choir.

JEAN. What church you go to baby?

MILDRED. Vernon.

JEAN. I know that church. It's down on Greenwood.

MATTHEW. I got to go back.

JEAN. Yes. I got to find my family

MATTHEW. I wish my brother was still here.

JEAN. I'm sorry.

MATTHEW. Well, I got to go back and get him. I got to at least make sure he has a decent burial.

JEAN. Family is so important. Without your family-

*(***MILDRED** *starts crying.* **MATTHEW** *and* **JEAN** *stop and looks at* **MILDRED**.*)*

JEAN. Mildred, baby, what is your last name?

MILDRED. *(whimpering)* Griffin.

JEAN. Griffin. I bet they're looking for you. Do you know your address?

(MILDRED shakes her head no.)

JEAN. Baby, I know they must be looking for you. Your Mama, Daddy, I bet you even have brothers and sisters.

MILDRED. I had four brothers and three sisters, but they all dead now. The white men killed everybody, but me. Sis told me to go hide and I hid under the bed. When I come back to where everybody was at, there was a lot of blood and nobody moved. I shook everybody. They are all dead. It's just me and Jesus now. Sis told me Jesus loves me.

JEAN. Yes, baby. Jesus does love you. That's why he sent you to Jean.

MATTHEW. Looks like Mildred done been through a whole lot. How old are you Mildred?

MILDRED. I'm nine.

MATTHEW. Well, Mildred. This uprising is hard on everybody. You a strong little girl. Jean said she gon' take care of you and I believe she will. I bet you hungry huh?

MILDRED. Yes sir.

MATTHEW. Yea, we all need to get something to eat. And right now, I don't see how we gon' eat in these woods. I stumbled across some plum trees last night. I fell over some plums on the ground when I was running. You like plums Mildred?

MILDRED. Yes sir. Well, I'll go and grab a few and come right back. Then, I got to go take care of some business.

JEAN. Why thank you Mr. Matthew.

MATTHEW. No problem.

(MATTHEW walks off stage.)

JEAN. Well Miss Mildred. I want to welcome you to your new family.

MILDRED. Ma'am?

JEAN. Well, I got a mama. We call her Big Mama. I got a husband and his name is Art. He's a strong man and works for the railroad. After he saved enough money from the railroad he started his own restaurant business on Greenwood. Even though he still works for the railroad he taught my two daughters Georgia and Grace to cook like his mama, and folks just loves their breakfasts, lunches and dinners. They especially love his chili. Georgia and Grace are gonna' love to call you their little sister.

MILDRED. How they gonna' do that when they don't even know me?

JEAN. They'll get to know you. You got any other kin that you know of?

MILDRED. No Miss Jean.

JEAN. Well, if you do we will see what we need to do. If not, we will work it out. Just know that God is gon' do what's best for Mildred. I hope everything has quieted down. We should start to head back soon. You will stay with me until we figure it all out.

(MATTHEW walks back and has a few plums in both hands. He hands two plums to JEAN and MILDRED.)

MATTHEW. Here you go. Eat on these. Miss Jean, and Miss Mildred it was nice meeting you, but I got to head on back to get my brother.

JEAN. Well, I hope you don't mind, we are going to stay here a while.

MATTHEW. Suit yourself.

(MATTHEW walks offstage, and JEAN holds MILDRED'S hands and says a silent prayer. After the quick prayer MILDRED watches MATTHEW leave as they eat the plums.)

End of Scene Seven

Scene Eight

(June 1, 12:00 noon. **BIG MAMA** *is downstage center laying by the tree stump as* **PAPA**, **TRESSIE** *and* **RUTH** *walk onstage.)*

PAPA. Let's rest here for a minute.

RUTH. These woods are pretty tough. I can't wait to get back on Greenwood. Lula Mae has got to do something with my hair. This country girl stuff is not for me.

*(***BIG MAMA*** rises and stands and points the gun at the three of them.* **PAPA** *raises his hands.)*

PAPA. Whooaaa, ma'am! We don't mean you no harm.

BIG MAMA. You can't just walk up on people like that. I'll be done shot you and turn around and ask God to forgive me.

PAPA. Ma'am. You ain't got to shoot nobody. It's just me and my two daughters. We running to safety from the white folks in Tulsa. I reckon you doing the same thing?

*(***BIG MAMA*** puts the gun down to her side.)*

BIG MAMA. Yes. That stupid son-in-law of mine might not be too stupid after all.

PAPA. Ma'am?

BIG MAMA. Name's Fairchild. Ethel Fairchild.

PAPA. Some kin to them Fairchild's that got that restaurant on Greenwood?

BIG MAMA. That's them.

PAPA. My name is Abe Taylor, and these are my daughters Tressie and Ruth.

TRESSIE. Nice to meet you Miss Fairchild.

RUTH. Same here ma'am

BIG MAMA. Pleasure to both of you.

TRESSIE. Did you have to run from the bullets too, ma'am?

BIG MAMA. Bullets?

TRESSIE. Yes, ma'am they were killing Negroes when we were leaving.

BIG MAMA. Well, I'll be damned!

TRESSIE. Ma'am?

BIG MAMA. I sent my grandboys back down there to see what was going on early this morning. I expect for them to be back anytime now. Their Daddy made us leave early yesterday evening in case there was going to be trouble. The car got a flat tire, so we camped out here for the night. We heard this big whistle and heard planes flying over our heads this morning.

RUTH. We heard it too. It seemed like we heard a bunch of guns going off like there was a war or something.

PAPA. Yes. And the smoke is getting worse these last few hours.

BIG MAMA. I can't stand not knowing what's going on. We need to know what our next move is going to be.

PAPA. That smoke seems like it is getting thicker.

(**LUVENIA** *walks in with* **BUD**.)

LUVENIA. Excuse me. I'm sorry I heard some folks talking and I thought I would come this way.

BIG MAMA. Come on in honey. I reckon you been running all morning?

LUVENIA. Yes ma'am. It was getting kind of scary where we were hiding. There were some army soldiers that came close to us, so we took to the bushes. As soon as they passed us, we started moving in the opposite direction. With y'alls talking, I knew you were colored folks, so I thought I'd better say something.

PAPA. What did you mean when you said army soldiers?

LUVENIA. Yes sir. These white men were in uniforms and had rifles and guns like they were in the army. We kept real quiet and they did not notice us.

BIG MAMA. You running by yourself child?

LUVENIA. Well, my husband, he-he was with us early this morning when they come in shooting Negroes and the airplanes was dropping bombs and killing coloreds. I saw my best friend and my cousin killed this morning for no reason. He took us to a shed that was on some property his Daddy owned. He went back to town to see if it was okay for us to come back. Well, my husband he told me to meet him at our

86

house if he didn't come back before the sun was about to set. We had to leave our hideout early 'cause of the soldiers. We were just headed that way when we ran into y'all.

BIG MAMA. Child, it seems like you done had more trouble in your life today than any of us have had. Why don't you come over here, sit down and rest a while?

(**LUVENIA** *sits on the tree stump as* **BUD** *limps along next to her.*)

TRESSIE. How did you hurt your foot boy?

BUD. Running from the bullets on the tracks.

TRESSIE. You must have been brave.

BUD. Yes'm

(**MOE** *and* **LEROY** *come in running and sweating. They are startled when they see all of the other people with* **BIG MAMA**. **RUTH** *notices* **MOE** *and walks towards him sexily.* **MOE** *notices her and smiles. He jerks towards* **BIG MAMA** *when she calls his name.*)

BIG MAMA. Moe!

MOE. Yes ma'am!

BIG MAMA. What is going on out there?

MOE. It is horrible Big Mama! Horrible!

BIG MAMA. Leroy! What did you find out?

LEROY. I don't know where to start Big Mama. It is all so bad.

BIG MAMA. Boy you better tell me something right now!

LEROY. They're killing us Big Mama. They're shooting colored folks on sight for no reason. We saw colored bodies everywhere. There were so many dead folks that the white folks started picking bodies up and putting them on trucks.

BIG MAMA. Putting bodies on the trucks?

PAPA. My God!

LEROY. Yes ma'am.

MOE. Yes ma'am, and we went down to the restaurant and it was-was-

BIG MAMA. Was what boy? Spit it out!

MOE. It was burned down Big Mama. It was all gone. The whole block was gone, and more stuff was burning. Then we saw-we saw-we saw-

(MOE starts crying and falls to the ground.)

BIG MAMA. What did you see boy? What did you see?

(LEROY goes over to BIG MAMA and turns her around to face him.)

LEROY. Grace and Georgia laying in the street shot to death.

BIG MAMA. NAW! NAW! THEM PECKERWOOD CRACKER SONS A BITCHES! NAW! NAW!

(LUVENIA gets off the tree stump and sits BIG MAMA on the tree stump. BIG MAMA sits down and starts rocking with her pistol still in her hand.)

PAPA. Maybe you ought to give me that gun.

BIG MAMA. No! I might have to use it!

LEROY. Big Mama there is more.

BIG MAMA. More boy?

LEROY. We ran into George Goodwin and he say that this young white boy, couldn't be more than thirteen years old shot the surgeon, Dr. Bridgewater, in the back and he had is hands up. Then they wouldn't even let nobody help him. Say he suffered and just bled to death.

(MOE gathers himself, stands and goes to BIG MAMA.)

MOE. See, the police are with the mob. They're pulling colored folks that stayed, out of their homes. If folks don't want to come out they were shooting them down. One man had his hands up and they told him to take off his hat. He goes to take off his hat and they shot him three times in the back.

LEROY. Then, we seen them marching the men folks to McNulty Park. We followed them by staying in the bushes. We were ducking and dodging behind houses and trees. One time we even had to hide in a chicken coop.

MOE. And you could tell that colored folks had already been hiding there, cause somebody had

to use the bathroom. Anyway, when we got out we saw another dump truck with nothing but bodies in it. We followed behind that truck. We were able to keep up with it because it kept stopping to pick up bodies.

LEROY. The truck finally stopped near Dawson Road, and we saw them dump bodies in a big hole. They were throwing lime on the bodies and it smelled real bad.

MOE. Leroy couldn't take it and he threw up. With him doing all of that gagging, we almost got caught. We had to get out of there quick.

LEROY. Then we saw white folks marching colored folks out of they houses. And when the colored folks were being taken by the police, another group of white folks would go in the colored folks houses and take all of their stuff. White folks was even taking pianos out and sitting them on a corner. They would come by in a flatbed truck and haul it off.

MOE. After they took everything they wanted out of the house. Then, they would burn the house up.

BIG MAMA. What about our house boy? Did they get to it?

LEROY. We don't know Big Mama. It was too dangerous to make it to our place. It was just too many white folks.

MOE. So, we followed where the white folks was taking the women and children. We saw them going into the convention center on Brady Street. And right after that we saw all of these soldiers get off the train and started heading north. But then we saw another truck picking up bodies. We followed it and saw three more trucks. They were going to the river. We tried to stay away from them and hid in the bushes. I climbed this tree and I was almost discovered because one of the men heard me in the bushes and started looking my way. I looked towards the Arkansas River and I saw dead bodies piled like stacks of logs. I saw black bodies being dumped into the river. The river looked like a river of blood. Then I looked back North, and I could see the soldiers caught some of the black men and they were taking them to McNulty Park.

LEROY. That was when I told Moe to come down. We had a hard time making our way back here, because with all the burning it wasn't too many places to hide. We hid behind a bunch of burning houses as we started to come back this way. We didn't want to get caught by the white folks, white folks police or the soldiers.

MOE. When we headed back we saw a lot of folks at Booker T. It seemed like that's where they were keeping the wounded cause the Red Cross was there.

BIG MAMA. Did you see or talk to anybody that might have seen your Mama?

MOE. No Big Mama.

BIG MAMA. *(to* **LEROY***)* What about your Daddy?

LEROY. No ma'am.

PAPA. You said Greenwood was burned down and they were robbing and looting houses.

MOE. Yes sir.

PAPA. These white folks don' went crazy!

RUTH. I was supposed to go to Booker T's prom tonight. I guess that's out.

 *(***RUTH** *looks at* **MOE***.)*

RUTH. I guess I'm going to have to find me another date.

 *(***MOE** *grins at* **RUTH***. She returns the smile.)*

TRESSIE. Girl, you need to stop being fast!

LEROY. Big Mama it was like the white folks couldn't believe that Negroes was living better than them.

BIG MAMA. That's them crackers. Hell, they got all of that oil money. Now they trying to steal what the colored folks done worked so hard far.

LEROY. Big Mama they were taking everything. And, from the looks of it, the police were helping them do it. They were not trying to protect the coloreds, they were-

BIG MAMA. Hush boy! Hush!

LEROY. But Big Mama-

BIG MAMA. Quiet!

 (A noise is heard in the bushes. Everyone freezes on stage. A voice is heard offstage)

OFF STAGE SOLDIER. Hey boys come this way! Look what I found!

 *(***BIG MAMA** *grabs her gun and draws it as* **LUVENIA** *grabs the gun and slowly hides it near the tree stump under a small bush.* **BIG MAMA** *looks at* **LUVENIA** *as the lights fade quickly.)*

End of Scene Eight

End of Act On

ACT II

Scene 1

(June 1, 1921 at 3:00 p.m. There is a fence covering stage right. There is a sign that says McNulty Park behind the fence. **JAMES** *is sitting on a bench.* **PAPA** *is sitting in a chair.* **MOE** *stands to the right of* **JAMES** *and* **LEROY** *stands to the left of* **PAPA**. **MOE** *and* **LEROY** *and are holding on to the fence.* **MATTHEW** *is pacing back and forth upstage of* **JAMES** *and* **PAPA**.*)*

PAPA. I wonder how long they're going to hold us?

JAMES. I don't rightly know.

PAPA. How long you been here?

JAMES. Since about 10 o'clock I guess. I was hiding in a hog pen for about two hours. I got lucky that the hogs didn't bother me. They kept quiet and I kept quiet. Then the militia came in and caught me. I was glad it was them instead of the police. I saw the police kill a colored man and he had his hands up.

PAPA. You got family?

JAMES. Yes sir. My wife and boy are out there by Mohawk. I told them not to come this way until close to sundown. When I left them they were safe? My Pops got a place out near Mohawk. He told us that it would be a good start for all of the grandkids. So far, I'm the only one that has stayed in Tulsa. My other brother went to Chicago and my sister married this ole' boy from Louisiana, and she went down there with him. I guess I got a lot to teach my boy as he gets older.

*(***MATTHEW** *screams loud in frustration. They all turn to look at him.)*

MATTHEW. AAAAAHHHHHHHH! This ain't right! This ain't right!

LEROY. Like we don't know that! Calm down! We need to figure out how we are going to get out of here.

PAPA. Leave the man alone son! Obviously, he's been through something.

LEROY. Like we ain't been through nothing! We are all suffering through this uprising. We need to try to stick together and all of us able bodied men need to do something. If I had a gun I'd-

PAPA. You'd do what boy! You'd do what?

*(**LEROY** gets quiet and walks away from **PAPA**.)*

PAPA. That's what I thought. Nothing. We have just got to wait her and hope that good minds prevail. From what we all have seen and heard this is a shameful day in Tulsa. With the soldiers here, they are obviously trying to protect us. We got to listen to them and hope the governor or the president will protect us.

JAMES. Yes sir. I seen what happened when we tried to protect ourselves. I saw some tough Negroes fight until they couldn't fight no more. We need to be proud of them.

LEROY. I ain't said I ain't proud of them. But how long are we gon' let them white folks treat us like slaves. When we gon' start sticking together and depend on ourselves. My Daddy always told me to respect my elders. But, I done looked all over this camp and I can't find him. All I can think is he's-

MOE. Don't say it Leroy! We don't know that!

LEROY. You saw all them dead bodies on that truck. You saw them bodies floating in the river. Was he with them? If he was, I bet he didn't just take off his hat and walk to this park with his hands up. If he fought like this man said, and how he saw Negroes holding white folks back on Standpipe Hill, then he died for something. He died so Negroes would have a chance to do better for themselves and their children. He died so, we wouldn't have to be treated like second class citizens. He died because he felt that the cause was more important than his life. Now tell me this-what are we going to die for?

PAPA. Son, I didn't become this old being no fool. We have to be wise. We have to see what we are working with, so we can move forward.

JAMES. The man is right son. We have to think and come up with a plan.

PAPA. It don't make no sense being all hotheaded and making the situation worse. Do you ever wonder why them soldiers didn't kill us? They could have killed all of us out there in them woods in Mohawk.

JAMES. They caught y'all in Mohawk?

MOE. Yes sir. They got all of us, him and his two daughters and this lady and her little boy.

JAMES. How old was the boy?

MOE. About 10 or 12. He had a rag on his foot. He said he cut it when they were running on the tracks.

JAMES. Where did they take them?

MOE. I don't know. I ain't seen them around here. They must have dropped them off somewhere. Them your people sir?

JAMES. Did the woman have on a white bandana?

MOE. Yes, sir. Must have been your folk.

JAMES. Yes. Sounds like my wife and son.

LEROY. Now what you gon' do? White man done took your wife and son. You ain't there to protect them. What kind of man are you?

JAMES. Watch your mouth youngin'. You don't have a right to talk to me like that.

LEROY. But, them white folks do, huh? Master Charlie can talk to us anyway. He been raping our women sense our folks came from Africa. Colored folks coming to Greenwood to make a different life for themselves. Now we down here, locked up like we are animals, and can't do nothing to protect ourselves, let alone our families. We need to bust out of here and start killing them, like they're killing us.

MOE. Leave him alone Leroy. He ain't done nothing.

LEROY. That's the problem. He ain't done nothing for nobody except himself. Where was he at when the Negroes went down there to stop them white folks from lynching Dick Rowland? And where is he now? He in here with us-waiting on what the white man is gon' do to us. What if the white man decides to lynch us, what we gon' do then?

PAPA. Listen to your brother boy. Now, cool heads have got to prevail. We have got to use our God given brains to work through this. We cannot start fighting against each other. If we do that, then we'll be falling right back into the white man's hands. We must stick together through this whole thing. Now, that white man could of killed us a long time ago like I said. But, for some reason, he didn't. Now, the white man ain't going nowhere. And, he knows he can't make it without us. That's why they keep coming down here and picking folks out, so they can go back to work.

MOE. Yes. I wish somebody would come and pull me out of this place. Daddy wouldn't let me work for the white man. All I could do was work at that chili parlor. Daddy always tell me that one day, I was going to be the owner of Art's Chili Parlor.

*(**MATTHEW** looks up when **MOE** says Art's Chili Parlor. He walks over towards **MOE**.)*

PAPA. We got to make sure that we do the right thing see-

MATTHEW. Excuse me gentlemen. I couldn't help but listen to your conversation. It is very interesting. But, I thought I heard you say something that sparked my mind a bit.

*(**MATTHEW** turns to **MOE**. He looks at **MOE** and then looks away.)*

MOE. Yes sir. You got something to say to me?

MATTHEW. Did you say your Daddy was the owner of Art's Chili Parlor?

*(**LEROY** steps in front of **MATTHEW** and postures himself to protect **MOE**.)*

LEROY. I'm his brother, who wants to know?

MATTHEW. Sir, I don't want no trouble. And I wonder if I. If I-I

LEROY. If I what mister? You got something to say-just say it.

MATTHEW. You sure your Daddy is Art from the Chili Parlor?

LEROY. You saw him mister?

MATTHEW. Yes sir. I saw him.

LEROY. He say something to you? Did he say where he was hiding out?

MATTHEW. I'm sorry to tell you this, but he's dead sir.

*(**MOE** falls on his knees).*

MOE. NO! Not my Daddy! Not my Daddy!

LEROY. Wait! How do you know it was him?

MATTHEW. Oh, I know Art. Knew him well. My brother and I used to eat there all the time. On a count of, well on account of his two beautiful daughters.

MOE. Daddy no! They killed my Daddy! They killed my Daddy!

*(**LEROY** starts to tear up a little. He is hurt and frustrated)*

LEROY. Tell me man. Tell me. What you see?

MATTHEW. I saw him shot dead when we were running. I knew it was him, cause me and my brother had just ate at the Chili Parlor before we went next door to Vadel's pool hall. He was telling Grace and Georgia there had been some trouble at the courthouse. We were walking out going to Vaden's when he walked in.

LEROY. DAMN!

MOE. *(continuing quietly)* My daddy! My daddy! My daddy!

(**LEROY** *walks away and puts his fist over his mouth.*)

OFFSTAGE WHITE VOICE. Is there a James Smith here? James Smith! Your employer is here to claim you boy! James Smith!

(**JAMES** *slowly rises. He walks over to* **LEROY** *who is in tears now.* **JAMES** *pats* **LEROY** *on the back as he exits.* **MOE** *is rocking back and forth on the floor.* **PAPA** *looks at* **JAMES** *and the lights fade to black.*)

End of Scene One

Scene Two

*(Outside the Convention Hall on June 1, 1921 at 4:00 p.m. There is a fence that covers an area stage left. It is very similar to the area that covers stage right. **BIG MAMA** is sitting on a bench inside the fence. **RUTH** and **TRESSIE** are standing together with their hands on the fence peering out.)*

BIG MAMA. I know y'all smelled all of that smoke when they drove us here in that truck. They didn't even take us through no parts of Greenwood.

TRESSIE. No ma'am they didn't. And when we got here the first thing they gave us was a bologna sandwich and some milk. I can't even drink milk. It makes my stomach turn.

RUTH. All of this stuff is turning my stomach. I was so looking forward to going to the prom tonight. I was going to wear this new blue dress that Leigh Griffin made me. I had tried it on two days ago and Leigh said that she just had to hem it.

TRESSIE. Ruth, when are you going to come out of la la land. Our whole lives have been turned upside down and all you can think of is Booker T.'s prom?

RUTH. I guess the other side is to keep thinking about this situation. When we were in the truck, besides all the smoke, there was this eerie death smell. It almost made me throw up.

BIG MAMA. Well, when we first got here, it was a joy and a shame to see that woman, have that baby.

TRESSIE. You were perfect. How long you been a mid-wife?

BIG MAMA. Girl, I been helping women bring babies into this world as long as I could remember. Them guards were watching so close you would think I was pulling a gun out from between her legs.

RUTH. Yes, it was so beautiful. I never seen nobody have a baby before.

TRESSIE. Yes, June 1, 1921 will be a birthday for the young boy that will always be remembered.

RUTH. I wondered where they were taking her and the baby.

TRESSIE. Probably Booker T. Remember how they had the Red Cross there when they dropped off that lady and her boy. What was they name's?

RUTH. She said her name was Luvenia and his name was Bud. She said her husband worked as a butler for some white folks and he was a good piano player.

TRESSIE. The boy had a pretty good cut in his foot. They probably was gon' get him doctored up. As bad as that foot was I hope he don't lose it.

BIG MAMA. Child, no telling. These crackers is crazy. They mess around and cut it off.

TRESSIE. You don't think they would-

BIG MAMA. These soldiers do look like they're trying to help. Now, there are some good white folks out there. I imagine many of them helped colored folks escape.

TRESSIE. Yes, ma'am we was some of them folks that white folks helped. I do appreciate Mr. Bell.

BIG MAMA. Baby, I never did catch your name.

TRESSIE. My name is Tressie.

RUTH. And, I am Ruth

BIG MAMA. Who are your people?

RUTH. We kin to the Goodwins.

BIG MAMA. The Goodwins that own all of them rent houses and business properties on Greenwood?

RUTH. Yes, that's my uncle J.H. Him and our Paw Paw are brothers. Uncle J.H. was talking last week about how them white folks' downtown were trying to get him to sell some of his property. He said he thought these white people were up to no good.

BIG MAMA. J.H. Goodwin. I know him real well. He was my landlord for a while, before I moved in with my daughter and her husband. Good man, Mr. Goodwin.

TRESSIE. Thank you, ma'am.

RUTH. I just hope. I just hope.

TRESSIE. Ruth, don't start.

RUTH. I am sorry Tressie. Ain't no sense in pretending. I know so far, we are the lucky ones. The way them boys was talking about what they saw. And then that-that death smell? Hmph! You know as well as I do everybody didn't make it. Some folks are dead. We just don't know how many of them is our kin people. And, we got to still find out if our house burned down. You saw all that smoke.

TRESSIE. I saw it, but it don't mean that it happened to us or our kin.

RUTH. It don't matter Tressie, it happened, and I can't take this.

BIG MAMA. How old are you baby?

RUTH. Nineteen.

BIG MAMA. Yes. You are just a baby. Just know, that if the good Lord is willing you got your whole life ahead of you.

RUTH. Ma'am

BIG MAMA. You're a Goodwin ain't you?

RUTH. Yes ma'am.

BIG MAMA. I've been knowing your people for some time and Goodwins are fighters. They don't let folks just misuse them and get away with it. I've known the Goodwins to get even, but they don't get even with their guns, they get even with their brains. What you got to do young lady is not let all of the shooting and killing worry you, 'cause you here. So far, you have lived to tell the story, and I hope you keep living so you can keep on telling it.

RUTH. Yes ma'am.

BIG MAMA. Now, I know I got a good judge of character. I see on the surface that you try to be a little fast sometimes, but you just teasing. Deep down, there is really a smart girl in there, that wants to make something of herself. If you could do anything you wanted to do in this world, what would you do?

RUTH. Anything?

BIG MAMA. Yes ma'am. Anything!

RUTH. I always wanted to be a newspaper reporter. I read every article that Mr. Smitherman writes in the Tulsa Star.

BIG MAMA. So be it! When we get out of here focus on being a newspaper reporter instead of men, and you just might get your wish one day. Mark my word.

RUTH. Like I wish I could have reported what I saw when we were riding in that truck. I saw Negro men with their hands held high. Then I saw colored women and children with their hands up being marched here to the convention center. There are just so many stories to tell and we need to tell our own stories.

BIG MAMA. That's right baby. 'Cause you better believe them crackers ain't gon' tell it like it should be told.

RUTH. I bet that Tulsa Tribune is reporting that all of this commotion is the Negro's fault. No matter what the real story is they find a way to tell a lie that people believe and run with.

BIG MAMA. Which is why we're sitting up here now waiting on them to decide when we can go home.

TRESSIE. I couldn't believe how them white folks was standing on the sidewalk cheering as our men were being marched somewhere.

RUTH. And how when we got off that truck they were grinning and clapping like somebody just hit a home run at a baseball game. These people really hate us colored folks.

(JEAN walks in and she is followed by MILDRED. JEAN notices BIG MAMA as she slowly turns around.)

JEAN. Mama?

BIG MAMA. Jeannie Mae?

(JEAN and BIG MAMA embrace each other very tightly. RUTH and TRESSIE grin and laugh for their happiness. JEAN and BIG MAMA separate and look at each other.)

JEAN. Mama, you are all right. Thank God! Have you seen Art? What about Grace and Georgia? Any word on Moe and Leroy? Oh Mama! It's so good to see you.

BIG MAMA. The soldiers took Moe and Leroy away from us. I hope they're some place like this. The last time I saw them they were mad, but they were okay. I ain't seen Art. I reckon when he told us to leave and run to the woods, he did the right thing. He said he was gon' get a hold of you and let you know. Did he ever talk to you?

JEAN. No Mama, I didn't hear from him. You know normally I always stop by the restaurant on my way home, but I couldn't get there with all of the shooting going on. I ended up coming home, the long way. I just thank God for leading me out of there. You know the bible say he will order your steps.

BIG MAMA. The bible. Yes, the bible.

JEAN. Mama you know I always keep my bible with me. But, I left so fast I left it on my bedside in my maid quarters.

BIG MAMA. Yes, I taught you how important it was to love God.

JEAN. You sure did. I remember we had to be in church every Sunday. But, when I was coming up, my favorite part about church was Sunday School. I guess that's why I like teaching it every Sunday.

BIG MAMA. Yes, I remember a few weeks ago you was saying how you was teaching about understanding or something.

JEAN. Yes, Mama I remember it was Proverbs 3:6. Where the bible say, "Lean not unto thine own understanding, but in all of thy ways acknowledge him and he will direct your path." Yes, Lord. He sure did direct my path running through them bullets.

BIG MAMA. Yes Jean, but we are going to really have to lean on his understanding.

JEAN. Yes ma'am,

BIG MAMA. Well Jean baby, ain't no easy way to say this. I guess I just got to say it.

JEAN. What is it Mama?

BIG MAMA. Well, baby, when we started hearing all the shooting and we saw a lot of burning, I sent Moe and Leroy to go back and see if they could see what's going on. Well, when they came back they saw some awful things.

JEAN. What type of things Moe and Leroy see Mama?

BIG MAMA. Well Jean, according to Moe and Leroy they saw Grace and Georgia, but they were both dead.

(JEAN slowly breaks down and starts crying very hard.)

JEAN. Dead Mama? What you mean?

BIG MAMA. They said they saw their bodies shot dead. I'm sorry. Jean baby. I'm so sorry.

(BIG MAMA starts crying.)

JEAN. No Mama. Not Grace Ann! Not Georgia Lee! MAMA NO! My girls, my girls, my girls! MAMA NOOOOOOOO!

(JEAN continues to cry very hard. She falls to the ground. BIG MAMA goes to her and grabs her and holds her on the floor. BIG MAMA rocks JEAN back and forth.)

BIG MAMA. I know baby, I know. Mama is here Jeannie baby, Mama is here. Mama here.

(BIG MAMA continues to rock JEAN as RUTH and TRESSIE watch her. MILDRED walks next to JEAN and puts her hand on JEAN'S shoulder as the lights

fade.)

End of Scene Two

Scene Three

(June 1, 1921 at 5:00 p.m. The lights come up center stage right at McNulty baseball park. **MOE, LEROY, PAPA** *and* **MATTHEW** *are still behind the fence. They are all eating beans.)*

MATTHEW. I tell you one thing, whoever cooked these beans need to take lessons from Art's Chili Parlor.

LEROY. Yea. That was one of my Daddy's favorite recipes.

PAPA. That's why white folks still need us. I ain't never known white folks who could cook. They'd starve to death without us.

MOE. I guess our boy who just left, must have had to go back to work. Do you 'spect they're going to call your name old timer?

PAPA. No son. This old timer don't work for the white man. I pride myself in working for myself. As a businessman, I believe it is important to invest. After working so hard on that railroad, my brother and I, J.H. Goodwin, we bought a bunch of rent houses and business properties. We do pretty good collecting monthly rents. We hire young folks like you and your brother here to work for us to do the handy work. I'm trying to keep my investments going to give my two girls an opportunity to go to college. My wife died about three years ago with that Spanish Flu. It was a tragedy.

MATTHEW. Sorry to hear that sir.

PAPA. Well, you learn to live with it. Just like we have got to learn to live with this. It was sad to see Mt. Zion Baptist Church on fire. I could see it from a distance. I know it was Mt. Zion based on the way the roof was designed. We worked hard to build that church.

LEROY. I just don't think we should just lay down and let these white folks do us any kind of way. We have been here all day. When are they going to let us out?

PAPA. Patience young man. Patience.

MATTHEW. I don't know mister. Oklahoma was supposed to be a place for colored folks to be free from all of this. I come from two families in Odessa, Texas that loaded up three wagons and drove all the way to Snake Creek. We drove day and night 'cause we were running from the Klan. We didn't stop until we got to Snake Creek because somebody heard that colored folks was settling there. In Snake Creek, all they talked about was Greenwood. So, me and my brother came up here figuring we could get a job at the railroad and then later, after we save our money, start us a business on Greenwood. We ain't been here but a coupla' months and all of this happen. What is that smell?

MOE. Same smell we been smelling all day.

PAPA. Get a good whiff son! Hopefully you will never smell it again. That is burning flesh.

LEROY. See! And we just sit here and let it happen!

PAPA. No son. We have to beat the white man at his own game. When the world hears about what happened on Greenwood, Tulsa, Oklahoma is going to feel the shame. From what we know right now, this is probably the biggest race massacre in the history of the United States. Do you remember what happened in Chicago?

LEROY. Chicago?

PAPA. Chicago. Boy, I bet you did not finish high school, did you?

LEROY. No. I started working shining shoes. I make good money. Didn't need no more schoolin'

PAPA. Well, I know they talked about it at Booker T. 'cause my niece came home talking about it. Anyway, they killed a lot of colored folks in the Chicago riots. And from my understanding there were riots in Washington, D.C. and Arkansas. Racial tensions was so high that white folks started killing Negroes for no reason. White folks got jealous of Negroes after they came back from the war. Negro soldiers was not given the respect they had over-seas. When they got back to these United States, they realized that nothing changed. After fighting for these white folks and risking their lives, white folks still called them all kinds of Niggers and treated them like second class citizens. I think history called them riots, "The Red Summer."

LEROY. So why we getting this history lesson old timer?

PAPA. Cause you need to know your history and where you came from, so you will know how to deal with it as you move forward. Don't be so hot-headed and be a damn fool. Think!

(MATTHEW pulls up a chair and sits.)

MATTHEW. Okay Old timer. School us!

PAPA. Let's start with our newspaper man from the Tulsa Sun Mr. A.J. Smitherman. I know you don't know who I'm talking about, but these two should know.

MATTHEW. I heard of him. They were talking about him in the pool hall the other day.

PAPA. Well, a few years back old Smitherman was supposed to be the colored folks' "Official Justice of the Peace." Well these white folks in Bristow, up the road west, was getting ready to lynch a young colored boy for whoever knows what reason. Anyway, you see Smitherman was in good with the governor. So, he contacted the governor and took three armed colored men with him to Bristow, and got that boy released.

MOE. How he do that?

PAPA. I don't know! All I know is he did it! Anyway, you know them white folks got mad!

LEROY. Sho' they did.

PAPA. So, they wanted Smitherman bad! And they got him!

LEROY. That couldn't be 'cause I saw him last week at Mann Brothers grocery store.

PAPA. Boy you don't listen well do you. Listen! They got him sho'. But, the only way they got him was a colored man set Smitherman up and they caught him! See that is what you got to think about. A lot of times, white folks won't fool with you. They will get some low-down, dirty-dog of a Negro, and pay that fool a few dollars to betray you. You got to watch your own kind. And sometimes, your own kind can be in high positions in the community, including those who preach about the good Lord every Sunday.

MATTHEW. Naaawwwww!

PAPA. Yes sir! Listen to me now! These folks, love money, more than they love their community and will sell you and everybody else out for less than twenty pieces of silver. Don't be no fool. I'm only telling you what I know. I don't even have to name names 'cause history gon' let you know.

MATTHEW. Did they ever catch the man who betrayed Smitherman?

PAPA. If I knew I wouldn't tell you. Do you read your bible?

LEROY. Bible?

PAPA. Do you read your bible?

LEROY. Uh-uh-uhhh-

PAPA. In your bible it says, "Vengeance is mine saith the Lord, and I will repay." And one day the white folks will have to pay for the shameful crimes they committed today.

LEROY. So again, what do we do?

104

PAPA. Wait on the Lord! He will guide you and show you the way.
*(**LEROY** walks away angrily from **PAPA** as the lights fade to black.)*

End of Scene Three

Scene Four

(Convention Hall on June 1, 1921 at 6:00 p.m. **JEAN** *and* **BIG MAMA** *are sitting on a bench.* **RUTH** *is sitting in a chair combing* **MILDRED'S** *hair as she sits on the ground.* **TRESSIE** *is staring through the fence.)*

BIG MAMA. Jean, you have got to stay strong. Just know that they are in a better place.

JEAN. I know Mama. I know. It is going to take me some time. Now, I got to hope and pray for who we know might be among the living. And that is, my husband Art, and my two boys Leroy and Moe.

BIG MAMA. I told you when the soldiers took us they took Leroy and Moe too. Now we all right. I am sure them boys are all right too.

JEAN. Lord, please take care of my husband and my boys. Please Lord.

BIG MAMA. God is good! It's going to be all right Jean.

TRESSIE. What church y'all go to?

JEAN. We are at Paradise Baptist.

TRESSIE. We go to Mt. Zion.

JEAN. Didn't y'all just build a new church?

TRESSIE. Yes ma'am. The church really worked hard to get it done.

MILDRED. Ouch!

RUTH. I'm sorry baby. It's a little nappy. I know how you feel, 'cause I'm a little tender headed myself. See, I need to take you to Ms. Hunt's the Creole Lady to make your hair grow. No, better yet, I need to take you to Madam Mabel Little, now she will get your hair silky smooth. Girl, have you ever been to a beauty shop?

MILDRED. No ma'am. Ouch!

RUTH. Well girl, when we get out of here, Miss Ruth gon' get you hooked up.

TRESSIE. Ruth, you need to stop all of that. This girl is way too young for what you got going on?

106

RUTH. What are you talking about Tressie? All girls got to learn to be a lady.

*(**LUVENIA** and **BUD** walk in. **BUD'S** foot is wrapped, and he is wearing some type of sandal on his wounded foot. The foot is wrapped as if he has gotten medical attention.)*

BUD. Hi Mildred.

MILDRED. Hi Bud.

LUVENIA. You all know each other. I thought y'all first saw each other in the woods.

BUD. Yes, Mama. But, Mildred is in my class at Dunbar.

BIG MAMA. How are you doing Ms. Luvenia? I want to thank you for your help earlier today.

LUVENIA. Ma'am?

BIG MAMA. Yes. I was about to shoot them crackers, but you pulled Roscoe out of my hand. I wasn't thinking wisely, and I could of got myself and everybody else killed.

LUVENIA. Well, I probably should have let you do it.

TRESSIE. So, the Red Cross fixed up your son's foot?

LUVENIA. Yes, they patched him up. I was so glad they were able to get to him, because it was a madhouse and other folks were in bad shape.

TRESSIE. Where there a lot of people there? Did you know anybody?

LUVENIA. I couldn't tell. It was so busy. Folks was screaming and yelling in pain. When we was waiting to get Bud treated, one lady told me that she saw a man tied to a car and they was dragging him down the road and shooting at him. Well, she said that he died. Then another lady said she saw one man come in and they had to cut his arm off. She said he was hollering so loud that the whole Red Cross heard him.

JEAN. Lord help.

LUVENIA. And then I saw two women who was in labor and both had babies. But, one baby was still born, and the nurse put the baby in a shoebox. The lady with the shoebox cried hard! You could hear her crying all through Booker T. They had so many people that they brought the lady out into the waiting room. She was tired and exhausted, but we saw the shoebox she was holding, and we knew it was her baby.

JEAN. How many men folk were there? Did you know Art from Art's Chili Parlor? Did you see him?

LUVENIA. No ma'am. I never been in the Chili Parlor and I don't know him, but there was a lot of men folk in there. The Red Cross was doing all they could to save them.

BIG MAMA. Jean, Jean. They're going to be all right. We are going to find them.

JEAN. But what if we don't Mama? I already lost my two girls. What are we going to do? Lord, please have mercy!

BIG MAMA. Jean where is your faith? I don't know nobody who talks about God as much as you. Where is your faith?

JEAN. I know Mama. I know. Art is just so much a part of this family. God knows we don't need to lose him.

BIG MAMA. Yes, I got to give it to him this time. He sho' saved my life yesterday. Had he not made us jump in that car and head north, I couldn't say we would be here today. And had we not had that flat, we probably could have gotten away like some of them other Negroes. I know some said they was driving to Muskogee. Other folks said they were heading east to Vinita. Some folks went west towards Sapulpa. All I know is if you didn't get out early you ended up running for your dear life. Whoo, these crackers done made the hair on my head stand up!

OFFSTAGE VOICE. Mary Pearson? Mary Pearson? Your white employer is here. You are welcome to leave.

BIG MAMA. I guess ain't none of y'all Mary Pearson huh? Ain't that something how white folks can't live without us? They didn't realize that after they kill us and take all of our belongings that they still need somebody to wipe the shit out of their babies' asses, and clean up after they ass? Ooo, these white folks done got on my last nerve.

OFFSTAGE VOICE. Is there a Jean Bryant here? Jean Bryant?

BIG MAMA. *(whispering)* Jean they calling you!

JEAN. I ain't going Mama. Y'all hide me. God's knows I might do something to that woman today if I go back to her house. Lord, please don't let me go. Please God, don't let me go.

> (**RUTH, TRESSIE, LUVENIA** and **BIG MAMA** hide **JEAN** as she sits on the bench with her head down between her legs.)

OFFSTAGE VOICE. Jean Bryant! Your white employer is here to pick you up! You are released to them now.

(RUTH, TRESSIE, LUVENIA and BIG MAMA continue to hide JEAN and act as if they are involved in deep conversation as they shake their heads no.)

OFFSTAGE VOICE. I'm sorry ma'am. We don't have a Jean Bryant.

(RUTH, TRESSIE, LUVENIA and BIG MAMA resume their positions on stage.)

JEAN. I am not going to the crazy white woman today! I have got to find my husband and my boys.

BIG MAMA. Them white folks really got their nerve. How in the hell do they expect somebody to come to work when they done lost their kin, can't find their kin and might not even have a home to go back to? You done took everything a person got. You're laughing at them and taunting them and then you expect them to act like ain't nothing happened. That has got to be the stupidest thing I ever heard of in all my born days. I just can't understand these crackers.

JEAN. Mama, Ms. Agnes is lost without me. I need another job. After my girls done got killed through all of this and I don't know where my husband is, and my boys might be alive or dead, I don't know. I just can't go to work today.

MILDRED. So, I won't get to meet my new sisters Georgia and Grace.

JEAN. No baby.

BIG MAMA. Ain't you going to find Mildred's people.

JEAN. Mildred say they all dead Mama. She said she saw all of them dead.

TRESSIE. Poor child.

MILDRED. I'm gon' be just fine. Miss Jean told me to stay strong 'cause Jesus loves me. Right Ms. Jean?

JEAN. That's right baby. Stay strong. Jesus loves you!

RUTH. Something is going on. Let me go see.

(RUTH exits off stage.)

BIG MAMA. When I get out of here, I have got to go find Roscoe. I might have to find me a way to kill some white folks. They have caused a lot of pain for one day.

TRESSIE. Yes ma'am. This is a sad day for Greenwood and Tulsa, Oklahoma.

(RUTH enters the stage.)

RUTH. They said they are going to let everyone go back home. They say that you must have a tag that says "Police Protection" or you will be arrested. Everyone is lining up to get released. Come on y'all let's go.

(They all exit as the lights fade to black.)

End of Scene Four

Scene Five

(June 1, 1921 at 7:00 p.m. **LUVENIA** *and* **BUD** *have a tag pinned on to their chests that clearly say, "Police Protection."* **LUVENIA** *walks around the debris of the burned home as* **JAMES** *appears.* **LUVENIA** *rushes to* **JAMES** *and hugs him as* **BUD** *grabs* **JAMES** *from the back with a hug.* **JAMES, LUVENIA** *and* **BUD** *freeze as the lights cross-fade to* **MATTHEW** *upstage center left. He is looking around for something and cannot find it. He falls on the ground and freezes as the lights cross fade center stage left to* **PAPA** *who is sitting on a rock in a burned area of the home.* **RUTH** *and* **TRESSIE** *enter from center stage left and hug* **PAPA. RUTH, TRESSIE** *and* **PAPA** *freeze as the lights cross fades to* **JEAN** *as she walks slowly to downstage center and notices the ruins of her house. She breaks down and starts crying heavily. She notices the bricks of the entry way of her former front porch. She walks over to the one side of the bricks.* **MILDRED** *and* **BIG MAMA** *follow behind* **JEAN**, *but they stay back as she cries.)*

JEAN. NOOOOOOOOOOOO! GOD NOOOOOOOOO! NOOOOOOOO!
    IT'S GOONNNNNEEEE LORD! IT'S GOOOONNNNEEEEEEEE!

*(***LEROY** *and* **MOE** *enter from upstage and hug* **BIG MAMA**.*)*

BIG MAMA. JEAN! JEAN!

*(***JEAN** *turns around and notices* **LEROY** *and* **MOE**. **JEAN** *runs to the both and gives them a big hug.)*

JEAN. MY BOYS! MY BOYS! Y'ALL ALIVE. THANK GOD!
    THANK GOD!

MOE. Mama! Mama!

JEAN. MY BOYS! THANK YOU JESUS! THANK YOU JESUS!
    Have you heard from your Daddy? Have you seen your Daddy?

*(***MOE** *turns his back and walks towards* **BIG MAMA**. *Then he turns around quickly to* **LEROY**. **BIG MAMA** *notices something is going on with* **MOE**.*)*

LEROY. Mama let's sit down on the stoop! I know you are tired.

JEAN. I'm all right Leroy. What do you know about your father?

LEROY. Well Mama, we don't actually know what is going on with Daddy.

JEAN. What are you talking about Leroy? Moe where is your Daddy? What have you heard?

LEROY. Mama, we don't know for sure. We need to make sure it was him.

JEAN. What is going on Leroy? Moe what happened?

LEROY. Somebody told us they saw him get shot.

JEAN. Shot? They shot him? Where is he at? Is it at Booker T. with the Red Cross? We got to go. We got to go.

LEROY. They say, he's dead, Mama.

(JEAN breaks down crying as MILDRED hangs onto BIG MAMA'S skirt. MILDRED also cries as she notices JEAN breaking down to the ground. MOE and LEROY can't take it and they go try to grab JEAN and slowly rise her to her feet.)

JEAN. MY HUSBAND! MY GIRLS! MY HOUSE! LORD PLEASE HELP ME! LORD PLEASE HELP ME! WHAT WE GON' DO LORD WHAT WE GON' DO!

(As JEAN sings she begins the song with LEROY and MOE holding her up. As the song progresses she finds the strength to step downstage and sing the song as LEROY, MOE, MILDRED and BIG MAMA look on.).

JEAN *(singing)*

Precious Lord
Take my hand
Lead me on
Let me stand
I am tired
I am weak
I am worn
Through the storm
Through the night
Lead me on
To the light
Take my hand
Precious Lord
Lead me home

(MILDRED walks over to JEAN and looks at her. JEAN grabs MILDRED and squeezes her tightly. MOE and LEROY walk over to JEAN and hug her and MILDRED. BIG MAMA walks slight down right and upstage of the four of them and turns and looks stage left, then stage right and then directly at the audience as the lights fade.)

End of Scene Five

112

Scene Six

*(This is the curtain call and it is a tableau. The lighting should resume a black and white photograph. No one should be smiling in the tableau and all characters are frozen. In the center of the stage, **JEAN** is seated in a chair and has **MILDRED** standing next to her on her left. **BIG MAMA** is sitting in a chair on the right of **JEAN**. **MOE** and **LEROY** are standing behind **JEAN** and **BIG MAMA**. **MATTHEW** is slightly upstage left center and looks off stage. Upstage right is **JAMES** and **LUVENIA**. **BUD** is standing in the middle of them.   Downstage left is **PAPA** in the center sitting on a tree stump or a rock and **TRESSIE** and **RUTH** are standing behind him.)*

End of Scene Six

END OF PLAY

Inspired by God

STORY THREE

GURLEY'S GLORIOUS GREENWOOD...GONE

CHARACTERS

HENRY JOHNSON is a 50-year-old butler. He is married to Helen.

HELEN JEAN JOHNSON is a 48-year-old married to Henry. She works as a maid for Tate Brady's wife.

SAMUEL CHANEY is a 40-year-old. His wife and son were killed in the race riot.

MAYOLA ANDERSON is a 35-year-old widow of a World War I veteran. She is a teacher at Dunbar Elementary School.

CHARLES FRANKLIN is a 25-year-old young man who wants to be a doctor.

MILDRED GRIFFIN is a 10-year old girl who is a student at Dunbar Elementary School. She is the niece of Henry and Helen Jean Johnson, and the only survivor of the Griffin family.

LEAUDRA HARRIS is a 70-year-old woman who loves her home and community.

JACOB HARRIS is the 40-year-old grandson of Leaudra. He is a newspaper writer and community activist.

MILTON GRAYSON is a 20-year old man who aspires to be a lawyer.

OLA FAYE is a 25-year old woman who works as a nurse for the American Red Cross.

JESSE ANDERSON is a 9-year old boy and son of Mayola Anderson.

Setting

Act 1

The early summer of 1921 in Tulsa, Oklahoma.

Scene 1

McNulty Park, June 2, 1921 at 7:00 a.m.

Scene 2

Booker T. Washington High School on June 2, 1921 at 10:00 a.m.

Scene 3

Outside the Harris' home on June 3, 1921 at 10:00 a.m.

Scene 4

Lawyer's tent on June 5, 1921 at 5:30 p.m.

Scene 5

Booker T. Washington High School on June 5, 1921 at 6:30 p.m.

Scene 6

The ruins of Greenwood Ave. on June 5, 1921 at 7:30 p.m.

Scene 7

Booker T. Washington High School on June 6, 1921 at 10:00 a.m.

Act 2

Scene 1

First Baptist Church North Tulsa on June 10, 1921 at 8:05 p.m.

Scene 2

Outside the Johnson's family tent in the morning of June 12, 1921 around 10:00 a.m.

Scene 3

The tent of the law offices of Franklin, Spears and Chappelle on June 13, 1921 at 10:00 a.m.

Scene 4

Outside the Johnson's family tent in the evening of June 13, 1921 at 5:00 p.m.

116

Scene 5

Outside the Johnson's family tent in the morning of June 14, 1921 at 8:00 a.m.

Scene 6

The tent of the law offices of Franklin, Spears and Chappelle on June 21, 1921 at 10:00 a.m.

Scene 7

Outside of the Johnson's family tent in the afternoon of June 25, 1921 at 1:00 p.m.

Scene 8

Curtain Call

ACT I

Scene 1

(Tulsa, Oklahoma, McNulty Park, June 2, 1921 at 7:00 a.m. In the downstage right area there is a fence and a sign in the background says McNulty Park. **HENRY, SAMUEL, CHARLES, MILTON** *and* **JACOB** *are standing behind a fence.)*

HENRY. Do you think they got anything else to eat besides beans? I been here for two days and all they seem to want to feed us is beans.

SAMUEL. Hopefully, they will let us out of here soon. It's hard not knowing what is going on out there.

HENRY. Whatever it is, it probably ain't nothing we want to see.

SAMUEL. I suppose you are right. When they picked me up in that chicken coop, I thought they was gon' kill me sho', like they did my wife when we both was running with the kids. I still see her, when her and my boy was ahead of me. I stopped to help George Mason and told them to keep running. George had a big gash in his leg from a gunshot wound. When I got George Mason up and put his arm around my neck we started walking together and he was limping pretty bad. All of a sudden, an explosion from out the sky hit my wife and my son. All I can think about is her and my son's body in pieces. I can't get her face out my mind. I wish they would have killed me instead of them.

(SAMUEL starts pacing back and forth and screams loud.)

SAMUEL. (continues) AAAAAAHHHHHHHHH! I WANT TO KILL THEM!

(SAMUEL starts to run off stage but is held back by JACOB who grabs him first. CHARLES and MILTON assist JACOB as SAMUEL struggles to get away.)

JACOB. Calm down, Sam! Calm down!

SAMUEL. Let me go! Let me go! I'm gon' kill 'em. I'm gon' kill 'em!

JACOB. Come on Sam! Come on!

SAMUEL. Take me! Take me! You sorry ass crackers!

(SAMUEL screams. His screams slowly become a cry, and then a whimper as he slowly calms down.)

JACOB. Easy, Sam. Easy.

SAMUEL. *(crying and sobbing)* Why did this have to happen, Jacob! Why! They killed my wife! They killed my boy!

HENRY. This here uprising have cost all of us Negroes. I just know that we have got to work hard to put all of this behind us.

(**SAMUEL** *is out of breath and slowly calming down.*)

SAMUEL. Tulsa ain't got to worry about me. If I ever get out of here, I ain't coming back. You can bet your last penny on that.

JACOB. We got to do what we can to help our people. Don't you get it. We are our only hope. If Negroes don't stick together, we will never have nothing. Whatever happens, I will do all I can to help our people. That man you helped with the big gash in his foot, did he survive with you?

(**SAMUEL** *is still out of breath.*)

SAMUEL. Yes, as far as I know. We were both in the chicken coop and the militia took him on a truck. I heard one of the guards say they were taking him to the school where the Red Cross was at.

CHARLES. That's what I wish I could do. I like to help people. I really wish I could go to school and study medicine.

HENRY. That's what we need young folks to do. They need to look out for our community. Whether it's a doctor, a lawyer, or a businessman. We need folks to want something out of life. That's how it is in my hometown of Boley, Oklahoma. My folks settled there years ago.

MILTON. Boley? Ain't that a town with all colored folks?

HENRY. Yes, sir. It is.

MILTON. Well, I want to be a lawyer?

HENRY. Good son. See Sam, it is important that these young folks look after us and give us hope for a future. What's you name son? And, who are your people?

MILTON. Name is Grayson. Milton Grayson. My folks come from the Creek Indians. My Pops was a Freedman. He died about three years ago. The fever got him.

HENRY. *(To* **CHARLES***)* And what about you, young man?

CHARLES. Name is Franklin. Charles Franklin. My folks came in with the Cherokee. We are Freedman too. Mr. Grayson, you say you want to be a lawyer, huh? Well, I got an uncle who is a lawyer. His name is B.C. Franklin. If he made it through this, I

119

will see if I can introduce you to him.

MILTON. Thank you, sir. I really appreciate that. I would like to get some ideas on what I need to do to study law.

SAMUEL. Well, well, well. What you say? We got boys that think they can be somebody. Well, look a here. Before you think you gon' be somebody, the first thing you need to do is figure out how to get out of this cage they got us stuck in and be a man. White folks don't want Negroes to be nothing. They come in our neighborhoods and kill us just for being Negroes.

JACOB. Come on Sam! We're going to come out of this.

HENRY. Let the boys think about how to help our people. We got to work together to figure this thing out. Now, we been here for two days. I'm sure, we will be out of here soon.

SAMUEL. *(To* **HENRY***)* You must not have seen what they did to Lee Johnson. Burned him up! He got tarred and feathered. Now you take that to your new doctor and have that one to lawyer it up! Them boys need to think about trying to get the hell out of here, before them white folks string us all up and tar and feather us too! You must be one of them white folks Negroes! Damn fool!

HENRY. Mind your peace boy!

SAMUEL. Mind yours!

*(***JACOB*** looks around the ball park.)*

JACOB. They even got women and children in here too. I ain't never seen this many Negroes in one place at the same time. This here crowd is bigger than they have at John William's Dreamland Theatre.

MILTON. *(looking around)* I was talking to Bill Williams a few minutes ago up in them bleachers over there. He is John Williams son, the owner of the Dreamland Theatre. He's a good friend of mine. He was telling me about how he and his Daddy was up in the Dreamland shooting down and killing white folks. He said them white folks couldn't figure out for where the bullets were coming from. Say his Daddy killed a whole lot of white folks.

HENRY. Yea. I heard that a lot of Negroes held them white folks off until that whistle went off. They say the army veteran O.B. Mann did a lot a damage?

SAMUEL. O.B. Mann?

HENRY. Yea, you know O. B. Mann. You can't miss him. Tall about 6 feet five inches. He's light-skinned from Mann Brother's Grocery store?

SAMUEL. Yea, I know who you are talking about. The army veteran. Yea, yea.

HENRY. Right! Say he was a sharp shooter that was good in the army. Say he killed a lot of Germans in the war and added a lot of white folks to that number on Greenwood. Say he was killing white folks from the buildings in Greenwood and then he went to help the coloreds at Mt. Zion. Say he's hiding out now, unless the white folks picked him up. I don't see him here, 'cause if he were here, you'd know it. But Jacob's right, Sam. I know it's tough right now. It's tough on all of us. At least you know what happened to your wife and son. We don't know what's going on with our families. We have got to stick together.

JACOB. I tell you what. It starts right here. Whenever we get out of here, we must promise ourselves that we will do whatever it takes to stick together. Even if it is just the five of us. That is a start. And, before you know it, we can build up this community again.

SAMUEL. Them Negroes went to the courthouse and stuck together for Dick Rowland and look what it got us. Sticking together don't mean nothing when white folks kill you and burn up everything you own. Not me! No sir! I am going as far away from Tulsa, Oklahoma as I can. I ain't got no family besides the ones I had. These white folks done took everything from me. As far as I'm concerned, if I ever get out of here y'all won't have to worry about seeing me as long as you live.

HENRY. Come on Sam. Give it some time. Give it some time.

SAMUEL. Tulsa, Oklahoma can go straight to hell!

> *(**SAMUEL** run towards stage right and **MILTON** and **CHARLES** grab him quickly. **JACOB** assists them and holds **SAMUEL** down as he falls to the ground.)*

SAMUEL. Let me go! Let me go! Let me go!

JACOB. Give us your word you ain't gon' do nothing stupid!

SAMUEL. Let me go! Let me go!

JACOB. Give us your word!

SAMUEL. You got it!

JACOB. Okay. Let him go.

> *(**SAMUEL** shakes **MILTON** and **CHARLES'** grasp away from him. They let him go. **SAMUEL** walks offstage angry, frustrated and hurt. **MILTON** and **CHARLES** look at **JACOB**.)*

JACOB. He'll be okay. He's just going through a tough time. You know, losing your family like that can be devastating.

HENRY. He ain't the only one who's had a hard time with this? I know how you all felt when you had to be humiliated and walked in here with your hands up. White folks laughing at you and calling you nigger this and nigger that. Hell, did you smell them dead bodies when that truck passed through here yesterday? We don't know if our families were in those trucks. And, even if it wasn't our folks, it must be somebody we know. We just got to figure this thing out.

MILTON. We'll figure it out Mr. Henry. But you know, I heard them soldiers say something about they were going to give us some cards so when our white employers come claim us, they can put us back to work for them. Then, the ones who don't work for the white folks they say they gon' pay all able-bodied men two dollars a day to clean up this mess. But, you got to pay for your own meals at twenty cents a piece.

HENRY. They done figured out they can't make it without us. Think about it. Who is going to take care of Mr. Brady's car when I am out? Who gon' get Mr. Brady some gas and drive him to work? See, as Mr. Brady's butler and chauffer, I am the one who he needs the most. It is only a matter of time that they call my name.

JACOB. You work for Tate Brady?

HENRY. Been working for Mr. Brady for the past ten years. My wife works for him as a maid. We got three children. Lucky for us, they were not here during this mess. My son is at Langston University. I got one daughter who is in Washington, D.C. at Howard and my eldest daughter lives in Chicago. I have not seen my wife since this riot, but I hope she is safe in the maid quarters at the Brady mansion. I am just praying she is okay.

JACOB. Ain't he that white man that got all of that oil money? They say he also a part of the Ku Klux Klan.

HENRY. And, how many white folks you know that ain't benefitting from oil money? And how many you know who ain't a part of the Klan? Hell, Negroes is benefitting from the white folks who making oil money. That's why we have been so prosperous in making this community in Greenwood successful.

JACOB. And whatever happens, we need to stick together and make it another success. But, we can't let them white folks keep running us over. We can't keep our mouths shut on this.

HENRY. You better keep your damn mouth shut if you want to stay alive fool!

JACOB. Who you calling a fool, Massa' Tate's boy?!

HENRY. Jacob, you better be glad I don't feel good, otherwise I will whoop your ass!

JACOB. You ain't no fool!

CHARLES. But all of the money did not come from oil sir as you claim.

HENRY. What are you talking about son?

CHARLES. Well, the majority of the land in Oklahoma, belonged to the Indians when they came here.

JACOB. You got some knowledge you need to share young man?

CHARLES. Yes sir, I told you that my parents were Freedmen. Well, at first, they were slaves and then they were set free with all the rights, land and money the Indians had. There is so much land in Oklahoma that belonged to the Indians that it is crazy. Land is money in Oklahoma. Some of them have sold it or have had it stolen. And, there are some that don't even know they have land that is there's to claim. My family owns a lot of land. And, my father is using that land as an asset for business. He lives in Muskogee and works the land with crops and cattle.

MILTON. He is right. I have heard my people talk about the same thing.

HENRY. Well, I stand corrected.

JACOB. That is why I am excited about you both wanting to do something for yourselves and make contributions to this community.

OFFSTAGE VOICE. Henry! Henry Johnson! Your employer Mr. Tate Brady is here to pick you up!

HENRY. Well, what did I tell you. You boys take it easy. I will see you in a little while. Remember, we got work to do.

JACOB. Just don't tell it to your massa', Henry.

HENRY. Don't be no fool! Fool!

     (HENRY exits.)

MILTON. *(To CHARLES)* So, you really think you can connect me with your uncle?

CHARLES. If he is still alive. I haven't seen him around here at this baseball park. But, another friend of mine said that they have some of us held up in other places like at the fairgrounds and the convention center.

MILTON. Well, I don't work for a white employer.

CHARLES. Neither do I. What about you Mr. Jacob?

JACOB. No sir. I work for Mr. A.J. Smitherman with the Tulsa Sun. I write articles and organize advertising and distribution for the paper. I have already been writing about this experience. As soon as I get out of here, you look for my stories.

CHARLES. Looks like the three of us will be working for that two dollars a day.

JACOB. I guess you right boy. Looks like they are trying to get started now. Everybody seems to be walking to some tables they are setting up. Let's go see what going on.

(The three men exit stage right.)

End of Scene One

Scene Two

(Booker T. Washington High School on June 2, 1921 at 10:00 a.m. A Red Cross banner hangs on the wall upstage center. There is a room with three make shift cots center stage. Three women are laying in the beds. **HELEN** *is in a bed center right.* **LEAUDRA** *is in the bed in the center and sitting up.* **MAYOLA** *is in the bed center left.* **OLA FAYE** *enters the room from upstage center.)*

OLA FAYE. How is Mrs. Harris doing this morning?

LEAUDRA. Girl, I don't know how many times I have told you to call me Leaudra.

OLA FAYE. Okay. I am sorry, Miss Leaudra. I was taught to respect my elders.

LEAUDRA. I am sure your parents taught you right. But, I told you and I told that doctor that I do not need to be in here. Ain't nothing wrong with me.

OLA FAYE. I know Miss Leaudra, but the militia said that something had to be wrong with you. They couldn't believe that you did not leave like the others. And when they found you sleep on your porch they thought you might have had a heart attack or a stroke.

LEAUDRA. I told you yesterday that when them white folks came to my house, that I was not leaving. I told them white men that they could take whatever they wanted and they would just have to kill me, 'cause I wasn't going nowhere. And I meant that. They knew I meant it too, 'cause they must have felt like this old lady is crazy. So, they turned around and left me alone.

OLA FAYE. So are you saying that you should be in the crazy hospital instead of the hospital for the sick and wounded?

LEAUDRA. You can say what you want to say. All I know is I ain't sick and I sho' ain't crazy. You need to give this bed to somebody who really need it. Tell that doctor to come in here. Now, if he gets too busy, I will move over there, get me a chair, and make sure you get somebody in here that needs this bed. Now, I done told y'all ain't nothing wrong with me.

OLA FAYE. Yes, ma'am.

LEAUDRA. Now what you say your name was? Ora, Ora...

OLA FAYE. Ola Faye.

LEAUDRA. Yes. That's right. Ola Faye. Well, look here Miss Ola Faye, is you married?

OLA FAYE. No ma'am.

LEAUDRA. Well, I got a grandson. His name is Jacob. He might be right for you? I've been trying to get that boy married for years. He acts like he can't do nothing but work for that newspaper and take care of his grandma. I love him to death, but that boy needs to have a wife and some kids. You like kids?

OLA FAYE. Yes, ma'am. But, I am too busy with my career right now. I just got out of nursing school and I love being a nurse. I've been working for the American Red Cross for about two years now.

(A scream is heard from **MAYOLA** *on* **LEAUDRA'S** *left.* **MAYOLA** *is sitting up screaming loud and looking frantic.* **OLA FAYE** *rushes to her aid.)*

MAYOLA. NO! MY BABY! MY BABY! MY BABY!

OLA FAYE. It's all right ma'am. It's all right ma'am. You're okay.

*(***MAYOLA** *starts crying very hard.)*

MAYOLA. (crying) My boy! My boy! He's gone! He's gone!

*(***MAYOLA** *tries to move and winces in pain.)*

OLA FAYE. Ma'am you have to be careful. Your thigh is hurt pretty bad.

MAYOLA. Was I shot?

OLA FAYE. Yes ma'am. You had to have surgery. The doctor took the bullet out. You are lucky that we did not have to take your leg. The doctor said you should be able to walk again, real soon. He said that you will be all right in a few weeks when the wound heals.

MAYOLA. But my boy! Do you know if he made it?

OLA FAYE. We don't know ma'am. When you came in you were unconscious and you had lost a lot of blood. What is your name ma'am?

MAYOLA. Mayola. Mayola Anderson.

OLA FAYE. Well, Miss Anderson. It is good to see that you are awake. The doctor will explain everything to you in more details. What do you do?

MAYOLA. I am a teacher at Dunbar. My husband died in the war. He started in October of 1917 at Camp Funston in Kansas as a part of the 92nd Infantry. He wrote me and say they called them the "Buffalo Soldiers Division" as a tribute to the four Buffalo soldier regiments that fought in the regular U.S. Army in earlier years. In February they sent him to France. He died on the front lines in August of 1918. He died serving this country. He was one of those three-hundred and eighty thousand Negro men who believed W.E.B. Dubois when he talked about how Negroes should show their patriotism by serving in the armed services to protect this country. He gives his life for this country and they turn around and shoot at his wife and his son? I got to find my boy. It's just me and my son, now. I got to be there for him. I got to.

LEAUDRA. Honey, I am so sorry to hear about your husband. He was a good man. Even though these white folks don't appreciate our colored soldiers, we do. Especially me. I seen first-hand how they treat our boys here when they came back. Army soldier in uniform need to go to the restroom at the courthouse and he got to go to the colored section. Veteran got medals all over his uniform and they not greeted with recognition of their civil rights, but, with hateful threats and hostile behavior from the very people they risked their lives for. I know two soldiers personally that still trying to get their disability for losing limbs. We gon' do all we can to help you find your baby. But, you 'bout scared us to death with all of that screaming. You got to be strong and keep the faith. The bible talks about that faith as small as a mustard seed. So, you got to get yourself well, so you can act on that faith. They say faith without works is dead. So, we got to help you go to work. If it's anything I can do to help you, my name is Leaudra Harris and I am member of First Baptist Church North Tulsa. If our church is standing or not, that's where you will always be able to find me.

MAYOLA. I'm sorry. It all just seems like a bad dream. We were running. I was holding his hand and he fell. He was screaming and crying in pain. The bullet hit him in the shoulder. He was bleeding pretty bad. I covered him up as we both were laying on the ground. I guess I must have passed out 'cause all I remember is waking up here. What hospital is this anyway?

LEAUDRA. Well, honey you are at Booker T. It was so many people hurt that the American Red Cross done turned this school into a hospital.

MAYOLA. Is my boy in this hospital? His name is Jesse. Jesse Anderson.

OLA FAYE. I will check ma'am. I will check.

MAYOLA. Thank you. I appreciate it.

(HELEN opens her eyes and slowly sits up on the side of the cot. Her back is to OLA FAYE, LEAUDRA and MAYOLA. HELEN looks straight ahead and does not notice anyone until OLA FAYE speaks.)

OLA FAYE. Good morning ma'am.

(HELEN turns to OLA FAYE and does not say a word. She has a bandage wrapped around her head. She turns her back to them and continues to stare ahead.)

LEAUDRA. You would think folks would have some manners.

OLA FAYE. It's all right. I'm used to it. Folks get cranky when they are in the hospital. What is your name ma'am?

(**HELEN** *ignores* **OLA FAYE.**)

LEAUDRA. Miss! Don't you hear this nurse talking to you?

(**HELEN** *is still silent.*)

MAYOLA. She might be a little nervous.

OLA FAYE. Yes. We will just give it some time.

(**CHARLES** *enters the room.*)

CHARLES. Hello everyone. My name is Charles. I am here to empty the trash and provide all of your cleaning needs.

OLA FAYE. Why thank you Mr. Charles. My name is Ola Faye Clark. It is a pleasure to have you work here.

CHARLES. The pleasure is mine, ma'am. So, you are a nurse?

OLA FAYE. Yes sir. I work for the American Red Cross. Mr. Maurice Willows is my Director. I came in with him from St. Louis.

CHARLES. Well, I was given the job to work here for two dollars a day. They had me held up for two days at McNulty with other men. They are paying all of us that don't have a white employer, two dollars a day to clean up after the uprising. I asked could I work at the hospital when I heard they were sending us out. I want to study medicine and become a doctor. I know that all I am supposed to do is empty the trash, sweep and mop floors, but I was hoping I could learn a thing or two about medicine. You think you can show me what you know Miss Ola Faye?

OLA FAYE. I'll do what I can, but you need to think about going to school before you go too far.

CHARLES. Yes ma'am. I am saving my money now.

MAYOLA. Sir, you said they had you held up with other black men at the fairgrounds? Did you see a young boy about nine years old out there?

CHARLES. It was a lot of folks, ma'am. Men, women, girls, boys of all ages. They came from all over. Most of us had been through a lot with this uprising and everything. Seems like everybody had a story to tell that wasn't too favorable about us colored folks.

I could have seen him, but I just don't know.

(HELEN stands up and starts walking downstage toward the audience. She turns and walks upstage of MAYOLA'S cot. She looks at LEAUDRA and then starts walking toward the exit door. OLA FAYE runs after her.)

OLA FAYE. Ma'am, where are you going? You cannot leave right now. Mr. Charles can you help me stop her from leaving.

(CHARLES tries to stop HELEN, but she breaks away from him. She runs out the upstage door and CHARLES and OLA FAYE follow after her. They catch HELEN offstage. CHARLES and OLA FAYE bring her back to the hospital cot. She sits reluctantly. When CHARLES and OLA FAYE let her loose she tries to get up again.)

CHARLES. Ma'am you cannot go anywhere. You are in the hospital.

OLA FAYE. He's right ma'am, please, you need to rest. That wound on your head is pretty bad.

LEAUDRA. What's your name baby? You look familiar. Who are your people?

(HELEN turns to look at LEAUDRA and starts crying. CHARLES and OLA FAYE let go of her hands and she puts both her hands to her face. She stands and walks downstage as CHARLES and OLA FAYE stand with her as LEAUDRA walks over to HELEN.)

LEAUDRA. What's your name baby? I have seen you somewhere. I just can't place it. It's gon' be all right.

(HELEN stops crying and wipes her tears. OLA FAYE gives her some tissue.)

LEAUDRA. *(continues)* My name is Leaudra. What's your name?

(HELEN shakes her head "no" and shrugs her shoulders. They all look at each other as HELEN stares at LEAUDRA, and the lights fade.)

End of Scene Two

Scene Three

*(June 3, 1921 at 10:00 a.m. **JACOB** steps outside a tent and sits in a chair. He has a sign on his shirt that says POLICE PROTECTION. He pulls out a tablet and starts writing. He looks up and notices **CHARLES** and **LEAUDRA** walking towards his way. He stops writing and stands.)*

LEAUDRA. Jacob! Jacob! Is that you, son!

JACOB. Mamadea' is that you?

*(**JACOB** runs to **LEAUDRA** and gives her a big hug. **LEAUDRA** and **CHARLES** also have signs on their chests that say POLICE PROTECTION.)*

LEAUDRA. My boy! My boy! You are all right! Praise God! Praise God!

JACOB. I was worried about you Mamadea'. When you said you were staying, I thought you might not make it out alive.

LEAUDRA. God was with me! They thought I was so crazy that they left me alone. Then another group of soldiers came through and the next thing I knew they had me strapped down in a cot and took me to Booker T. with the Red Cross. They said I was passed out, but still breathing. They thought I had a heart attack or something. Lord knows, I fell asleep. Anyway, I am blessed to be talking to you right now. God is good!

*(**LEAUDRA'S** happiness to see Jacob slowly fades away as she looks around.)*

LEAUDRA. *(continues)* This is what is left of our house and community huh? I see when they packed me off of that porch that they decided to burn up the house. Lord have mercy! You were born in this house. Your Mama Evelyn's last words when she had you was take care of him Mamadea'. I knew the best way to make sure that you was raised right was to have a house for you to live in and always come back to. It's gon' now. The Lord give it and the Lord take it away. Blessed be the name of the Lord.

JACOB. We'll be all right Mamadea'. The main thing is that we are both alive. We will rebuild this house right here on this lot and it will be better than before!

LEAUDRA. *(looking around)* Yes, but a big part of my life was in this house. All of my personal items. Pictures of your Mama, some of her things, memories, all gone. Little things. Things are gone that I never did want to part from. You don't miss it now, but it will hit you later.

JACOB. *(To **CHARLES**)* Thanks for seeing to it that my grandmother got home.

CHARLES. No problem, Mr. Jacob.

JACOB. Charles, right? Well, I hope you keep that dream of yours alive and become that

130

doctor.

CHARLES. I am working on it sir. Good to see you again Mr. Jacob.

JACOB. You too young man.

LEAUDRA. Y'all two know each other?

CHARLES. Yes ma'am. They held us up at McNulty Park. We got to spend a little time together.

JACOB. So, you getting a chance to work in the hospital, huh?

CHARLES. Yes sir! I'm doing clean-up and maintenance, but I get to learn to read medicine a little. I know it's just a matter of time and I will get a chance to learn more. But, my goal is to go to school. The hospital wanted me to set this tent up for Ms. Leaudra before I come back.

JACOB. Much obliged sir, but I can take care of it.

CHARLES. Are you sure? It's part of my job. I have been putting tents up yesterday and today. It really wouldn't be a problem. What did they end up getting you to do?

JACOB. They got me cleaning up what's left from the buildings. You know them white folks burned out about thirty-four-square blocks of homes and businesses. They gave me this sign and say, I got to wear it at all times or I will be arrested. They say I got to make sure, I report at 7:00 a.m. every day or face consequences.

CHARLES. You see my sign too, don't you?

JACOB. Don't worry about the tent son. I'll put it up. Maybe it will give you a little bit more time to study medicine.

CHARLES. Ok, then. Good to see you again, Mr. Jacob. I am going to get back to the hospital. Take care, ma'am.

(**CHARLES** *drops a bag on the ground as he leaves.*)

LEAUDRA. They give me one of these tents here too at the Red Cross. Well, I guess we can use both of them for a while. I am glad I kept this insurance up on this house. We need to file a claim and get this house rebuilt before winter time come.

JACOB. Mamadea' I have already been looking at that and I just hope we don't have no problems.

LEAUDRA. What type of problems are you talking about boy?

131

JACOB. Well, Mamadea, I been reading what these white folks is talking about in the paper. First of all, their saying that the Negroes started this uprising. Look at this Mamadea, the Tulsa Ministerial Alliance say here in the Tulsa Tribune that "The fair name of the city of Tulsa has been tarnished by the ranks with the dastardly deeds of the Germans during the Great War, provoked by the bad element of Negroes, arming themselves and marching through the streets of the city.

LEAUDRA. The only marching I see Negroes doing was with their hands up. And if they took them down, they would be shot in the back. I saw Luther Green get shot right over there when he came out of his house.

JACOB. I know Mamadea'. Look here. They go on to say that "Acres of ashes lie smoldering in what but yesterday was "Niggertown."

LEAUDRA. No boy!

JACOB. Yes ma'am. They say block after block of our city had been swept by fire applied by the frenzied hand of the mob.

LEAUDRA. They must be talking about the white mob.

JACOB. No ma'am. They say "Many of our colored people are dead, while thousands of innocent, peaceable, and law-abiding white citizens have not only been rendered homeless, but have been robbed and despoiled of all their earthly possessions.

LEAUDRA. They must be talking about what happened to colored folks.

JACOB. They say, "The pastors of Tulsa blush for shame at this outrage which renders our city odious and condemned before the world.

LEAUDRA. I can't see why people write that type of nonsense. And folks actually believe that stuff?

JACOB. The Tulsa Tribune is always mixing the truth with lies Mamadea'. That's how them lies sell papers. They give you a little bit of truth and mix it up with a bunch of lies. See, at the Tulsa Sun, we spend a lot of time correcting those lies and try to give colored folks an opportunity to see what is really going on. If we don't tell our own story, the white folks story will go down in history and whatever they say, folks will believe it as the truth. It is important that we tell the story from the way we see it Mamadea'!

LEAUDRA. Well, before we do anything, we have got to figure out how we are going to survive. Now, the Red Cross has given us a few items, but we are gon' have to get creative and work some things out around here.

*(**JACOB** looks offstage right and gazes as if he is looking in a distance.)*

JACOB. I wonder who is that man walking this way.

LEAUDRA. What man? I don't see no man.

JACOB. He seems to be passing something out to the folks in that tent over there. When that young man Charles was here, I saw him earlier from a distance.

LEAUDRA. Oh, I see him. Wonder what he is passing out?

JACOB. Well, we are going to find out soon enough. Here he comes.

(MILTON walks in from stage right. He is dressed in a suit, tie and a hat.)

MILTON. Mr. Jacob is that you sir?

JACOB. Yes, sir it is. And who are you?

MILTON. Sorry sir. I guess you probably don't recognize me in this suit and hat.

(MILTON takes off his hat. He shakes JACOB'S hand. JACOB shakes his hand back reluctantly and LEAUDRA gazes at MILTON with a look of suspicion on her face.)

JACOB. Don't reckon I do.

MILTON. Well sir, let me refresh your memory. It was only a few days ago, that they had us locked up at the fairgrounds. Remember there was this guy named Charles who said he wanted to be a doctor?

JACOB. Ironically, he just left here.

MILTON. Well, I was the guy who wanted to be a lawyer.

(JACOB recognizes him.)

JACOB. *(happily)* Yea! Yea! I'm sorry. I remember now. I told the both of you boys to go for your dream. Charles just told me that he is working at the hospital. He is a janitor now, but he said he is going to be studying up on medicine.

MILTON. Yes sir! Well, he introduced me to his uncle B.C. Franklin. And, Mr. Franklin and his partners, Mr. Spears and Mr. Chappelle hired me as a part-time Legal Aid. I am going to get a chance to learn law from some of the best lawyers in the city. I only get to after I finish my new day job cleaning up this rubble. I try to work for the lawyers as much as I can.

JACOB. I do that too. I guess we do the same thing, we're just on separate crews. That's good

133

son. That's good. What's your name again son? I am bad with names.

MILTON. My name is Milton. Milton Grayson.

JACOB. Well, Mr. Milton Grayson. Let me introduce you to my grandmother, Mrs. Leaudra Harris.

MILTON. Nice to meet you Mrs. Harris.

LEAUDRA. Call me Miss Leaudra.

MILTON. Miss Leaudra.

JACOB. Well, son. What are you passing out to folks around here?

MILTON. Well, Mr. Jacob, like I said I am working for the law offices of Spears, Franklin and Chappelle. And they are already working on helping colored folks like yourself who have lost almost everything in the uprising. And by the look of the tents, they were reaching out to folks in the community to let them know that they are working together to make sure that if you want to stay in Tulsa that you get an opportunity to rebuild.

JACOB. Keep talking boy! What you're saying sounds pretty good so far.

MILTON. Well, this law firm is looking at this situation from a legal perspective. They know if it was just one or two Negroes fighting for their rights it would be hard. That's why they are trying to get Negroes to work together on this. Now, I remember what you were saying Mr. Jacob when we were at the park. You were a strong advocate for colored folks working together. Well this is an opportunity to do just that. This here handbill is just to let you know that Spears, Franklin and Chappelle have set up a tent similar to the one you got. They will talk about this in detail if you like. Just use the information on this bill here if you are interested.

JACOB. Okay son. My grandmother and I will take a look at it.

MILTON. That's all we are asking Mr. Jacob. I appreciate you taking the time to talk to me. I am going to move on and talk to as many folks as I can before it gets too dark. I appreciate your time. Ma'am.

(**MILTON** *walks off stage left.*)

JACOB. All right son. Much obliged.

LEAUDRA. What you thinking son?

JACOB. I was about to ask you the same thing Mamadea'.

LEAUDRA. Well, it seems like it might be worth at least checking it out. Why don't you go down there and see what they talking about?

JACOB. Well, it won't hurt to see what is going on. Let me get you settled and I will go down there.

LEAUDRA. I can find my way around this tent. You go ahead and see what them lawyers is saying. You can see from what you read in this newspaper that them white folks ain't up to no good. Colored folks need a lawyer to help them through this legal stuff.

JACOB. Okay, Mamadea'. I am going to head that way.

LEAUDRA. Helen. Helen Johnson.

JACOB. What did you say Mamadea'?

LEAUDRA. Henry Johnson's wife.

JACOB. I saw Henry in that camp. He says he works for Tate Brady.

LEAUDRA. Well, you see if you can catch up with Henry. Tell him his wife is at Booker T. in the Red Cross Hospital. I wonder if he knows.

JACOB. Yes ma'am. I don't know if he does.

LEAUDRA. Helen Johnson.

(*JACOB walks off stage right.* **LEAUDRA** *goes into the tent as the lights fade.*)

End of Scene Three

Scene Four

(June 5, 1921 at 5:30 p.m. There is a tent that is open to the audience. The tent has two chairs on the right of a small table and one chair on the left of the table. This table serves as a desk. Upstage of the tent is another small table with four chairs. **MILTON** *is sitting with his back to the audience at the table with the four chairs.* **HENRY** *walks in from stage right.)*

HENRY. Hello sir?

*(***MILTON*** turns around and notices ***HENRY***.)*

MILTON. Mr. Henry! How are you doing?

HENRY. Milton is that you?

MILTON. Yes sir!

HENRY. Maybe I got the wrong tent. I got this flyer from a Mr. B.C. Franklin and Mr. A.J. Spears. I saw them yesterday when they came through my neighborhood. They say they are lawyers and they want to help us colored folks that lost everything to come to their office and discuss how they can help us. They said to look for a flag on their tent on this street. I saw the flag, but I see they are not here, so I must be mistaken.

MILTON. You're not mistaken Mr. Henry. This is the right tent. Remember me telling you that I wanted to be a lawyer?

HENRY. You did say that you wanted to be a lawyer, didn't you?

MILTON. Well, Mr. Franklin and Mr. Chappelle, hired me on the spot. I told them I was interested in being a lawyer and I wanted to learn more. Well, they told me I wouldn't make much to start, but they hired me as a part-time legal assistant.

HENRY. What you say?

MILTON. Yes sir! And I am learning a lot too!

HENRY. Well, what time do you expect them back?

MILTON. Unfortunately, all three of them said they would not be back today. They said they wanted to spend the last couple of hours recruiting folks for the lawsuit. Most of us are working, you know. They got me cleaning up rubble. I get off at 5:00. I got a little tent like this on Kenosha.

HENRY. That's why I come down here to see exactly what they are talking about. What you know about all of this? Maybe you could shed some light on this situation.

MILTON. Yes sir, I can-

*(JACOB walks up to the tent and interrupts **MILTON**.)*

JACOB. Gentlemen! Gentlemen! It is good to see the both of you again. I am just glad it is under different circumstances.

HENRY. Yes sir, Jacob! It is hard, but from the looks of things around here, most of us have lost everything.

JACOB. Yes, that's why when Milton gave me and mom this flyer yesterday, I come over here to check it out. I came by later yesterday, but I couldn't find anybody.

HENRY. Milton was about to tell me what this is all about when you walked up. Go ahead Milton, we all want to know what this is about?

MILTON. I wish the lawyers were here to tell you more details, but I can tell you what I know. The law firm of Franklin, Spears and Chappelle want to make sure the Greenwood area residents and business owners get what they need to rebuild their homes and businesses. According to the law firm the city wants to take the land for themselves and work on some other project.

HENRY. I don't plan to go nowhere!

MILTON. That's what the lawyers have said they have heard from most of the people who were burned out.

HENRY. Everybody on my block that I have talked to have said they are going to rebuild.

JACOB. I wish I could say that too. But, Sam lives a few doors down and he is dead set on getting out of Tulsa as soon as possible. And it's a lot of folks talking about getting the hell out of here. Some of them say if they build it back, the white folks are going to do all they can to tear it down again.

MILTON. Well, I know Mr. Chappelle said he is trying to get the community to come together to make sure everything is ready to rebuild, but he said he is running into resistance. He said that there are several white leaders in the city who are trying to make sure that the Negroes don't get a chance to rebuild. He said they will try to come up with anything to stop us. He said they are coming up with some type of ordinance that says in order to build in this area you have to have steel beams and stuff. We know Negroes don't have that kind of money. We just hope that the Negroes stick together.

HENRY. *(thinking out loud)* Wait a minute.

JACOB. Hold up Milton. We have a white folks Negro in our presence.

HENRY. Go to hell Jacob!

JACOB. Then what are you thinking about Henry?

HENRY. I heard Mr. Tate Brady in his office with three other white men talking about some sort of fire ordinance coming to Greenwood. I was minding my business as usual and Mr. Brady call for me to bring him a box of cigars. When I get there, he tells me to give one to each of the three men. I didn't catch their names, but I am sure, I would remember them if I saw them or heard their voices. Mr. Brady asked them to smoke up in celebration of the new fire ordinance. Could that be what they are planning to do?

JACOB. You know how white folks do? I know you work for Brady, but a lot of folks say he says one thing and does another. Say he hires a lot of colored folks to work for him and goes on like he really likes us. Then, he wears that Ku Klux Klan robe at night and go about terrorizing colored folks. I don't trust Tate Brady. I wouldn't work for him if he paid me three times what he's paying you. Why you keep working for the man?

HENRY. Ah Tate Brady a good man to work for.

MILTON. He ain't too good if he trying to stop folks from re-building on their own property.

JACOB. Do the lawyers have anything to say about the insurance? Do they think we are going to get to claim our loss?

MILTON. Well, I do know that Mr. Franklin has really been working on that situation. He was saying that he had already started calling several insurance companies and they are all saying the same thing.

JACOB. Come on boy! What are they saying?

MILTON. Well, what they're saying is that they need a report from the governor's office to determine who is at fault on this situation. They say if it was outsiders who did this deed then everybody would get their claims. However, if it is determined that Negroes caused this uprising, then most of the claims in the colored community would be denied. The governor say he's is waiting on the Grand Jury's report.

HENRY. Well, I'll be damned! You know that these white folks gon' play crazy like they always do? You know they gon' blame this on Negroes. We might as well start trying to build on our own.

JACOB. Wait a minute Henry! There you go. Don't give up too easy. Wait a minute. I picked up a paper earlier and I thought I saw something about how these white folks were going to help us rebuild. Wait a minute. Hold on a second. Yea! Here it is. Listen to this. It says that the Tulsa Mayor T.D. Evans was in a meeting with the Chamber of Commerce and he said "The rest of the United States must now know that the real citizenship of

Tulsa weeps at this unspeakable crime. And we will make good the damage so far as it can be done, to the last penny.

HENRY. They know they really messed up. At least they are feeling sorry for what they did.

JACOB. *(continues reading)* We have neglected our duties and our city government has fallen down. We have had failing police protection here, and now we have to pay the costs of it. The city and county are legally liable for every dollar of the damage which has been done. Other cities have had to pay the bill of race riots, and we shall have to do so, probably, because we have neglected our duties as citizens."

MILTON. That's why the lawyers are working so hard to make things right for black folks. I do know that Attorney Spears is working with the governor's office and the police to determine who was at fault.

JACOB. Determine who was at fault! We already know. You see they are admitting that it was their fault. But, you see these white folks think they are slick. Just yesterday, I read this in the Tulsa Tribune.

HENRY. Man, why are you walking around with all of these newspapers?

JACOB. That's what I do Henry. I am a newspaper writer. It is my job to see what the white folks are saying so I know how to tell the colored folks what we need to do. White folks believe this stuff and they act on it. Otherwise, we wouldn't be in the situation we are in now.

HENRY. We wouldn't be in this situation if Negroes wouldn't get all riled up about a young Negro messing with a white girl.

JACOB. Let me read it to you, Henry so it ain't no question.

HENRY. I'm listening. I'm listening.

JACOB. *(reading)* This is June 4, 1921. The title says "IT MUST NOT BE AGAIN. Such a district as the old "Niggertown" must never be allowed in Tulsa again. It was a cesspool of iniquity and corruption. It was the cesspool which had been pointed out specifically to the Tulsa police and to Police Commissioner Adkison, and they could see nothing in it. Yet anybody could go down there and buy all the booze they wanted. Anybody could go into the most unspeakable dance halls and base joints of prostitution.

MILTON. I wonder where they are getting their information from? You do not see too many white folks on this side of town. And why do they have to call our community "Niggertown?"

JACOB. *(continues reading)* All this had been called to the attention of the police department and all the police department could do under the Mayor of this city was to whitewash itself. The Mayor of Tulsa is a perfectly nice, honest man, we do not doubt, but he is guileless. He could have found out himself any time one night what just one preacher found out.

HENRY. What is a white preacher doing in our community at night?

JACOB. In this old "Niggertown" were a lot of bad niggers and a bad nigger is about the lowest thing that walks on two feet. Give a bad nigger his booze and his dope and a gun and he thinks he can shoot up the world. And all these four things were found in "Niggertown"-booze, dope, bad niggers and guns.

HENRY. That's how they put it? But, I thought you just said they was gon' help us?!

JACOB. That's what the Mayor said-

HENRY. But, if he said that, then you mean to tell me the white folks don't want that?

MILTON. Boy! Them white folks are something else. That's why you need a lawyer!

JACOB. You ain't heard the half of it. Let me finish! The article goes on to say that "The Tulsa Tribune makes no apology to the Police Commissioner or to the Mayor of this city for having pleaded with them to clean up the cesspools of this city. Commissioner Adkison had said that he knew of the growing agitation in "Niggertown" some time ago and that he and the Chief of Police went down and told the Negroes that if anything started they would be responsible. That is first class conversation but weak action."

MILTON. Why do they have to come over here and clean up our part of this city? They need to look at what they are doing instead of focusing on colored folks.

JACOB. Now listen here, 'cause here they go. "Well, the bad niggers started it. The public would now like to know: why wasn't it prevented? Why were these niggers not made to feel the force of the law and made to respect the law? Why were not the violators of the law in "Niggertown" arrested? Why were they allowed to go on in many ways defying the law? Why? Mr. Adkison , why? The columns of the Tulsa Tribune are open to Mr. Adkison for any explanation he may wish to make.

HENRY. Apology? Respect for the law? Sometimes I think white folks are crazier than they look.

JACOB. *(reading)* Those bad niggers must now be held accountable, and, what is more, the dope selling and booze and gun collection must STOP. The police commissioner who has not the ability or the willingness to find what a preacher can find and who WON'T stop it when told of it, but merely whitewashes himself and talks of "knocking chairwarmers" had better be asked to resign by an outraged city."

MILTON. They already blaming Negroes for this. How are we going to get justice in this situation?

HENRY. From the way you talking this legal stuff is just a blow in the wind. Don't look like these lawyers gon' be able to do nothing. When do you say they will be back?

MILTON. Like I said, they will not be back today.

HENRY. Oh, you did say that.

JACOB. Well, I can't stay right now. I got to find Mr. A.J. Smitherman and see how he wants to report this? I was told he is still alive and in Tulsa.

HENRY. Jacob are you talking about the Tulsa Sun?

JACOB. Of course, what else could I be talking about?

HENRY. Man, it's gone! Everything is gone! How are you going to print a paper?

JACOB. I don't know. But as soon as I find Mr. Smitherman, we are going to figure something out. I'm gone!

(*JACOB starts to leave and then suddenly stops.*)

JACOB. Henry, I came by what I thought was your tent yesterday, but you were not there. I figured you were probably at the hospital with Helen.

HENRY. Helen is in the hospital?

JACOB. I thought you knew. My grandmother told me she saw her at Booker T. with the Red Cross-

(*HENRY runs off stage as JACOB turns to MILTON.*)

JACOB. (*To MILTON*) I guess he didn't know.

(*JACOB walks offstage as MILTON sits at the table. The lights fade to black.*)

End of Scene Four

(June 5, 1921 at 6:30 p.m. **HELEN** *is standing downstage center of the bed looking towards the audience. The middle bed is empty and is made up neatly.* **MAYOLA** *is sitting up in her bed reading a book and facing stage left.* **OLA FAYE** *walks into the room and* **HENRY** *follows her.)*

OLA FAYE. Good morning Miss Mayola. How are you this morning?

MAYOLA. I am doing much better ma'am, thank you.

OLA FAYE. Good! Good! And how do you feel this morning ma'am?

*(***HELEN** *turns around and faces* **OLA FAYE.** **HENRY** *enters the room and notices* **HELEN** *as she turns around. He walks over to her quickly. He grabs* **HELEN** *and hugs her happily and she breaks away from him and goes towards* **MAYOLA.** **HELEN** *is scared and looks confused.)*

HENRY. Helen what is wrong? I am just so glad to see you and know that you are alive.

*(***HELEN** *looks at* **HENRY** *like she does not know him. She is very afraid and confused.)*

HENRY. *(continues)* You look well. Are you feeling good? You know I have been worried about you something fierce.

*(***HELEN** *looks at* **OLA FAYE** *and* **MAYOLA.** **HENRY** *looks worried. He looks at* **OLA FAYE.** *)*

OLA FAYE. Mr. Henry, I'm sorry, but these head injuries can be very serious.

HENRY. Helen talk to me. It's Henry. Your husband.

*(***HELEN** *looks at* **HENRY** *and does not respond.)*

MAYOLA. I don't think she knows who you are sir.

HENRY. Helen talk to me.

OLA FAYE. Mr. Henry. I'm sorry. She hasn't said a word since she's been here.

HENRY. Do you know what happened to her?

OLA FAYE. No sir! All we know is when they brought her in, she had a big gash on her head. We treated it the best we could. Physically she is okay. But, now that you said that she does not know you. Plus, with her not talking. Obviously, there is something else wrong?

HENRY. I need to talk to her doctor.

(**HENRY** *walks towards* **HELEN**.)

HENRY. *(continues)* Helen. Don't you remember. It's me honey. Henry.

(**HELEN** *shakes her head no.*)

OLA FAYE. Mr. Henry. Maybe you should leave for now. I will let the doctor know that you want to see him. Ms. Helen really needs to get some rest.

HENRY. All right. I will be waiting. Helen, I love you.

(**HELEN** *does not look at* **HENRY** *as he exits.*)

OLA FAYE. Ms. Helen. You really should be laying down, honey. You need your rest.

(**HELEN** *walks over to her bed and sits down.*)

HELEN. *(stuttering)* I-I don't know him. He said-he said-he my-my husband. But, I-I- don't know him.

MAYOLA. Praise the Lord, she is talking.

OLA FAYE. How are you feeling right now?

HELEN. *(stuttering)* I-I feel-feel okay. My head-head hurts a-a little.

MAYOLA. Well, Miss Helen. It is good to hear you talk. Do you remember anything?

HELEN. *(stuttering)* I remem-remem-remember running. I-I-I don't know why-why I was run-run-running, but I was-was run-run-running.

OLA FAYE. These things take time. Sometimes your memory is slow to come back. Maybe you should just lay down.

(**OLA FAYE** *goes to* **HELEN** *and helps her to the bed.*)

HELEN. *(stuttering)* Every-every-thing-thing seems like it's just-just a-a a blur.

MAYOLA. Ms. Helen, things have been rough on everybody. The doctor says I can leave today, but first, I got to find my boy! I got to check this hospital again and see if anyone might have seen him. I wish things could get back to normal. I heard the school burned down.

OLA FAYE. Yes. But, I'm sure there's a lot of children who still need schooling.

MAYOLA. Yes, I miss my babies. But, I miss my son more than anything. I sure hope he is okay.

(MAYOLA starts whimpering and then crying.)

OLA FAYE. Don't fret yourself so now. We just have to keep looking. Doctor says you will be out of here soon. That should give you more time to look for him.

MAYOLA. *(crying)* I got to thinking though while I was laying on this bed that he might not be alive. I got to find my boy.

(OLA FAYE hugs MAYOLA and she wipes the tears from her cheeks.)

HELEN. *(sitting up and stuttering)* Can y'all-y'all tell me what-what happened? How-how did I get-get here? Why-why do I think I-I-I was running from some-something? That man-man-man that was here. Why-why he-he say he-h my husband? I don't-don't know-know him.

OLA FAYE. You just need to rest Ms. Helen. The doctor will be here to see you soon and maybe he can give you some answers.

HELEN. I-I am just so confused. I-I don't know what to-to do.

OLA FAYE. Rest Ms. Helen. It will be all right.

(HELEN lays down as OLA FAYE helps her to lay down. OLA FAYE stares at MAYOLA and then walks out of the room. MAYOLA looks at HELEN as the lights fade.)

End of Scene Five

Scene Six

(June 5, 1921 7:30 p.m. **SAMUEL** *is sitting in a chair center stage. He is wearing a tag that says, "Police Protection." He rises and looks towards stage left and just stares ahead for a moment. Then he shakes his head and walks towards stage right and stares ahead. He falls on his knees and starts crying like a baby.)*

SAMUEL. It's gone. Everything we worked so hard for is gone! I'm sorry Rose. I'm sorry.

*(***JACOB*** enters from upstage left and calls* **SAMUEL***)*

JACOB. Samuel! Samuel! Have you heard about the lawyers?

SAMUEL. What lawyers? What are you talking about?

JACOB. They've been passing out these hand bills. You know, Buck Franklin, Chappelle and Spears are trying to help colored folks clean this mess up and rebuild. They already have things in motion for colored folks to get some of that insurance money and start putting our community back together. We got to get this thing back to the glorious days when Booker T. Washington came here. He called the Greenwood area the "The Negro Wallstreet." Lots and lots of Negroes saw this as the promised land.

SAMUEL. Don't be trying to sell me no dream Jacob. O.W. Gurley's glorious Greenwood is gone. You didn't talk to him in that camp like I did. You should have seen his face when he was telling me what happened to him.

JACOB. Gurley was in the camp? I didn't see him.

SAMUEL. 'Cause he did not want to be seen. He tried to hide himself as much as he could, but I knowed who he was, 'cause I know his walk. I lived in one of his rent houses, and that house was right here and as you can see it is ashes. He told me everything 'cause he had to. He says he knowed it was up to him to let me know what happened to my boy and Rose. He says he saw them laying in the street in pieces when he was running. Course, I knew he was telling the truth.

*(***SAMUEL*** starts to whimper again and cry.)*

SAMUEL. *(continues).* My Rose. My Rose. I gon' miss my Rose. And little Jim use to tell me all the time that he was gon' work on the railroad just like his Pappy. But, they both is gone now.

JACOB. You know the Red Cross is passing out tents and supplies to folks, so you can have some shelter.

SAMUEL. Don't need to Jacob. Gurley told me everything.

JACOB. Did he tell you how he tried to convince the colored folks to not go to the courthouse? Did he tell you that all he was interested in was saving his own business interests instead of protecting the rights of all the Negroes in this community. Did he tell you how he-

SAMUEL. No Jacob! It wasn't nothing like that! For the first time in my life I saw Gurley as a Negro just like you and me. He was beat down real bad, just like me right now. I was feeling just like you until he said what he said.

JACOB. What did he say?

SAMUEL. First, he talked about how when all of this stuff started he was at the Gurley Hotel with his wife, Emma. Said he figured when the white folks started attacking that he could go over there to them, him and Emma and they would recognize that he was a Negro of stature and they wouldn't harm him. Well, he said he was wrong, 'cause as soon as he walked over there toward them white folks, they started shooting at him and Emma. He said they started running and Emma got hit by one of them bullets and fell on the streets. He went to her and she told him to run on without her. With bullets still coming he took off and left her lying there. He told me that after everything happened he wished he would have took a bullet and lay next to her. He said when he was running and the bullets were flying he knew he was just another Nigger to them white folks. They didn't care who he was or what he meant to the Negro community.

JACOB. Yea, one thing you can't take away from O.W. Gurley was he started Greenwood. He turned that little store of his into a community when he began to sell and rent land out to folks. He built the first hotel. He is a true businessman alright. I guess he will probably join the rest of us and start to rebuild and bring Greenwood and this community back to where it used to be.

(SAMUEL starts shaking his head no.)

SAMUEL. Gurley say his fifty-three-year-old legs ran as fast as they could north on Greenwood. He said he passed some folks, but he had to get off Greenwood and he ran east and took shelter in a crawl space at Dunbar Elementary School. He said he sit there for what seemed like hours thinking about how these Negroes done messed up his life with Emma and his businesses. He felt like if them Negroes wouldn't have went down to that courthouse none of this would've happened. He said every now and then he would peek out of his crawl space and see Negroes running. He say then, they slowly stopped. He saw a whole lot of white folks walking the streets. He said they came to where he was hiding and he heard a white teenager say, "He crawled in right there, and I saw him. I saw him." He said he saw the barrel of a rifle come in the hole and they fired the rifle several times. He said one time the bullet just grazed him and he almost screamed. Then he heard them say that he must have went out the other side. He said a few minutes later he heard a lot of glass breaking and he realized that the school was on fire. He knew he had to get out 'cause he could die from the smoke. He heard the noise quieted down and the white mob ran further north away from the school. He said he crawled out and went towards the front of the school where he saw an old white man holding about fifteen Negroes. He said he threw up his hands and after a while they took them all to that camp we was at.

JACOB. I didn't even know that Gurley was at that camp where they held us up.

SAMUEL. He was there.

JACOB. Well, I wonder what is he going to do now?

SAMUEL. I don't know. But, he told me that when they was taking them to the camp, he saw my wife Rose and my son Jim on one of them trucks dead.

JACOB. Are you sure he said it was them?

SAMUEL. That's what he said. He knew them. And he would see Lil' Jim all the time. He said, he didn't think my son had legs on him. He's telling the truth. I saw 'em.

JACOB. Everybody knows Gurley. Always wearing that bow tie. But, this thing ain't over Samuel. We got to stick together and work this thing out. You know white folks are plotting. They already blaming this uprising on the Negroes.

SAMUEL. That's why I'm leaving. Some Negroes got all the luck in the world no matter how the white folks do them.

JACOB. How can you say that Samuel? I can't think of one Negro that didn't lose something in all this.

SAMUEL. I'm talking about O.W. Gurley.

JACOB. I know they burned up all of Gurley's property. And from what you just told me Gurley even lost his wife.

SAMUEL. So, I thought. Right after Gurley told me about Rose and Little Jim, his wife shows up at the park. Turns out she just fainted and thought she was hit. She's fine and Gurley is a happy man once again. I guess it goes to show that material things don't mean nothing when you got family and loved ones.

(**SAMUEL** *starts to break down again.*)

SAMUEL. *(continues.)* I can't do it Jacob! I can't do it! All I can think about is Rose and Little Jim. I got to get out of here! I got to get out of here!

(**SAMUEL** *starts to walk off.*)

JACOB. So, you are just going to leave?

SAMUEL. Hell, I ain't the only one Jacob! Most of the Negroes I have been talking to in that camp and all over town. They talkin' about getting out of here. Ain't no more promised land in Tulsa. These white folks done shot and bombed us to death. Took anything of value from our homes and then burned them down. Now, they got the Red Cross come in here and feel sorry for us. Like we something they care about? Come on, Jacob!

JACOB. But we've got to show them Samuel. We've got to show them that we can stand up to them.

SAMUEL. How are we gon' do that Jacob? I know you read the paper about how they have blamed everything on the colored folks? But, I am glad some of us colored folks had the nerve to stand up to the white folk's foolishness. But, face it Jacob, it ain't gon' get no better? James Johnson, Leroy Alexander, Hap Watson, Daniel Black. Hell, almost everybody I know except you talking about getting out of here. Most of them are already gone. Hell, I bet A.J. Smitherman is gone too. Most folks talking about going North or Northeast, 'cause they ain't got time to do no sharecropping in Mississippi in Alabama for these white folks.

JACOB. So, the strong colored folks are going to run away from it?

SAMUEL. Hell, they fought them as long as they could Jacob? The white folks just took it to another level and came in strong and overpowered the Negroes. We were not ready for this.

JACOB. I don't understand why leaving and not still fighting is the best thing to do.

SAMUEL. Lot of folks ain't gon' have nothing but bad memories about the last few days Jacob. I lost my family, they put our dead kinfolks, neighbors, church members in these mass graves and you want to make peace with them and rebuild this community. To hell with that, Jacob! That's why I'm with the majority of colored folks who gon' take this damn sign off that say "Police Protection" and get my ass outa' here! And, if you had any sense, you'd get that grandma' of yours and keep it moving! It ain't nothing in this here white town of Tulsa, Oklahoma that would make me and most of the Negroes who got sense stay here. You can stay if you want to and keep pleasing massa', but I'm gone. Gone, gone, gone!

JACOB. Where are you going?

SAMUEL. I don't know. Chicago. Washington, D.C. North. Somewhere as far away from Tulsa, Oklahoma as I can go.

JACOB. I wish I could change your mind.

SAMEUL. I got to go Jacob! You take care of yourself. GONE!

(**SAMUEL** *snatches off the Police Protection tag and throws it to the ground, looks at*

148

JACOB *and runs offstage.)*

JACOB. Bye Sam.

*(***JACOB*** looks after* **SAMUEL** *and turns and walks upstage as the lights fade).*

End of Scene Six

Scene Seven

(June 6, 10:00 a.m.   Booker T. Washington High School. Red Cross Hospital. **HELEN** *is sleeping on her bed stage right.   The other two beds are empty.   The bed next to* **HELEN** *is not made, but the bed stage left is made.* **CHARLES** *enters the room and is followed by* **OLA FAYE**. **CHARLES** *is carrying a small female child and he takes the child to the bed stage left.* **OLA FAYE** *pulls back the covers and* **CHARLES** *lays the girl in the bed.   The small girl is asleep and has a bandage on her foot.* **OLA FAYE** *pulls the cover over the young girl.* **CHARLES** *and* **OLA FAYE** *try not to wake up* **HELEN** *by whispering.)*

OLA FAYE. She's going to be all right now.   Boy, talking about a screaming child.

CHARLES. Yea, that glass falling on her foot from that busted window must have hurt pretty bad.

OLA FAYE. For the glass to cut through her shoe, I know it hurt.   The doctor says it will take a while to heal, but she's a tough little girl.   She should be able to go home in a couple of days.

CHARLES. So why does it have to be a couple of days?   How come she can't go home now or why not two or three months Miss nurse?

OLA FAYE. The doctor wants to make sure that it does not set up any type of infection. If it heals the way it should, she should be okay.

CHARLES. See, I am learning.   I really want to learn how to be a doctor.   I appreciate you calling me to give me an opportunity to learn as much as I can.

OLA FAYE. Well, if you really want to learn, keep working with Dr. Bridgewater as much as possible.   Let him know you want to learn and he may give you more opportunities to assist.

*(***HENRY** *walks in talking in a normal tone.)*

HENRY. Hello ladies and gentlemen!

*(***OLA FAYE** *motions for him to whisper by putting her index finger to her lips.)*

OLA FAYE. Sssssshhhhh!   They are sleeping.

HENRY. *(whispering)* Ohhhhh!   I am sorry.   I will keep it down.

CHARLES. Good to see you Mr. Henry.

HENRY. The pleasure is mine Dr. Charles.

CHARLES. Well, you know I am working on it.

HENRY. *(to* **OLA FAYE***)* Do you mind if I just wait here for a while?

OLA FAYE. No sir, go ahead. I'll be back after I make the rest of my rounds.

(**OLA FAYE** *and* **CHARLES** *exit as* **HENRY** *walks towards* **HELEN** *and just stands over her for a few seconds.* **HELEN** *wakes up and sits up and looks at* **HENRY***.)*

HELEN. Henry?

HENRY. How you doing Helen?

HELEN. My head hurts.

HENRY. You just take it easy. You are getting better!

HELEN. *(looking around)* I'm in a hospital?

HENRY. Something like that.

HELEN. I remember running. Oh, white folks shooting and killing. Folks dead, bullets, bombs, Henry, no!

(**HELEN** *get excited and loud and frantic.* **HENRY** *hugs her as she starts crying.)*

HENRY. It's okay Helen, it's okay. It's going to be all right! It's going to be all right.

HELEN. Henry you are okay! You are alive! We are alive! Thank God! Thank God!

HENRY. Yes, baby! Everything is good! We are all right! We are all right!

HELEN. How long have I been here?

HENRY. Just a few days.

HELEN. What they say is wrong with me?

HENRY. They said that you took a hit to the head. You didn't remember me since you been here. They said you had amnesia, but they didn't know how bad it was. Thank God you remember me now. They said it might take a little time for you to remember things.

HELEN. I want to get up.

HENRY. Here. Let me help you.

(**HELEN** *gets up and takes a few steps.*)

HELEN. Henry, it seemed like the end of the world.

(**HENRY** *goes to her.*)

HENRY. Don't talk about it baby. Don't talk about it!

(*The little girl in the bed starts to turn over and moans a little.*)

HELEN. They must have brought this patient in when I was sleep.

HENRY. It looks like a child.

(*The little girl sits ups and rubs her eyes and looks at* **HENRY** *and* **HELEN**.)

MILDRED. Hi Uncle Henry and Aunt Helen.

HENRY AND HELEN. MILDRED?

(**HENRY** *and* **HELEN** *look at each other and then at* **MILDRED** *as the lights fade to black.*)

END OF ACT I

ACT II

Scene 1

(June 10, 1921 First Baptist Church North Tulsa. 8:05 p.m. **JACOB, LEAUDRA, HENRY, MILTON,** *and* **MAYOLA** *are coming on stage. They are dressed casually, and* **JACOB** *walks out ahead as they walk to the center of the stage outside of the church.* **MAYOLA** *has a cane and is limping.)*

JACOB. It is just hard to believe what we just heard in there.

HENRY. Jacob, you got a lot to learn.

LEAUDRA. Well, they said the man told his side of the story.

JACOB. Yes. I know that! But, I was there. And that is not the way it happened.

HENRY. We all came to this community meeting of colored folks here at First Baptist Church of North Tulsa to see how we need to come together. We got to forget about all of this and rebuild our city.

MILTON. I understand Mr. Henry, but it is hard to move forward if you don't resolve what has happened in the past.

MAYOLA. Mr. Franklin's report about the Grand Jury Trial was interesting.

JACOB. That's what I can't get past. Can you believe the nerve of O.W. Gurley?

HENRY. The man is just doing what he got to do?

JACOB. Doing what he got to do? See Henry, you don't get it. This is the problem that we have in this community. It's Negroes like you and Gurley who need to go.

HENRY. I am just a little more stable than you are Jacob. I think we need to just keep our noses to the grindstone and work hard to rebuild what we lost.

JACOB. Okay. I understand that! But, we need to get our rights in the process.

LEAUDRA. These white folks ain't gon' give us nothing Jacob! We can't sit around here waiting on them to give us some money to rebuild what they tore down in the first place. They not thinking about us. I agree that we need to just move on and cut out all of this foolishness about getting money from them insurance folks, 'cause they gon' find any way they can to not give it to us.

JACOB. But, Mamadea', do we have to do it to ourselves? Do we have to blame our own people for how the white folks did us? Why do we have to tear each other down? Why do we, as a people, must hurt one another instead of helping each other.

MILTON. Yes. Mr. Gurley's testimony in front of the Grand Jury was devastating to the Negroes cause.

HENRY. Mr. Gurley is a leader in this community son. He has a lot of property in this community and has built it up to where it is?

MILTON. Well, with all due respect Mr. Henry, it is all ashes now!

HENRY. That's why we got to rebuild it. We got to make it better than it was before-

MAYOLA. Now according to the Grand Jury report, Mr. Gurley said that A.J. Smitherman, O.B. Mann and John Williams started the riot. Mr. Gurley said that at Smitherman's newspaper office, Smitherman led them Negroes down to courthouse. He said that O.B. Mann provoked the white folks and John Williams organized Negroes from his Dreamland Theatre to go kill some white folks.

JACOB. Then Gurley said that on the night of the riots he went to the newspaper office about nine o'clock and found activities advanced.

MAYOLA. *(reading a newspaper)* According to the report Gurley said, 'in answer to the call to arms, guns and ammunition were being collected from every available source. Many of the men were making open threats and talking in a most turbulent manner."

JACOB. He was talking about how when he saw what was going on and how he tried to talk them out of the idea of arming themselves to prevent what they believed was threatened lynching, but they were in such a dangerous mood that he got troubled. He even had the nerve to say they were nearly all dope users and drinkers with police records. I have no respect for Gurley. All he thinks about is himself. His testimony caused the Grand Jury to say that the Negroes started the whole thing. And, if the Negroes started it then-

MILTON. That means the Negroes will not get any help from the insurance companies. But, does that give the City of Tulsa any right to go back on its promise to help black folks rebuild?

JACOB. Not when you got Henry's boss, Mr. Tate trying to say that the only way we can build on our own land is to have steel. How many Negroes you know can afford steel?

LEAUDRA. Jacob that's why we got to lean on each other. We got to work together to rebuild our community step by step.

JACOB. I have got to find Smitherman. We need our leadership back. What you all are talking about is letting the white folks get away with this. We cannot do that!

HENRY. You know he's hiding out-just like them others that Gurley pointed out. If them white folks catch them, they all just as good as dead!

JACOB. If I could just talk to him, though. I need to know for myself.

HENRY. A.J. Smitherman is probably long gone by now. As well as the rest of them. The white folks done run them out of town. We have got to work with these white folks and rebuild our community.

JACOB. Well, I'll tell you who really needs to go, and fear for his life too.

MILTON. Obviously, you are talking about O.W. Gurley. And you are right. They say him and his wife left town right after his testimony. I don't think we will see Mr. Gurley for a while.

(**HELEN** and **MILDRED** walk into the scene.)

HELEN. Henry! We are ready. The children had a good time this evening. How did the meeting go?

HENRY. Well, it—

MILDRED. (To **MAYOLA**) Hi Miss Anderson!

(**MILDRED** runs to **MAYOLA** and gives her a hug.)

MAYOLA. Hi Mildred! It is so good to see you. How are you doing?

MILDRED. I'm doing fine! How is Jesse and his arm? I saw him at that place and his arm was all wrapped up?

MAYOLA. You saw Jesse?! You saw Jesse?!

MILDRED. Yes ma'am. He was looking for you. Did you find him?

(**MAYOLA** starts crying and hugging **MILDRED**.)

MAYOLA. Mildred, I need you to tell Ms. Anderson exactly where you saw Jesse at you hear me?

(**MILDRED** starts to get nervous. She looks at **HELEN** and back to **MAYOLA**.)

MILDRED. I saw him at that place where we was locked up in a fence with big buildings. He said he got shot. I told him that I almost got shot too. He say that he was looking for you. Then, this white man in a army suit grabbed his other arm and told him to go

155

with him. I did not see him after that.

MAYOLA. Oh, Mildred! Thank you so much! Thank you so much! My baby alive. He's alive. Now, Mildred how is Robert and the rest of your family?

*(**MILDRED** starts crying. **MAYOLA** is slightly taken aback. **MILDRED** cries harder and **HELEN** walks her offstage as **HENRY** looks at **MAYOLA**. **MAYOLA** looks at **HENRY** with a look of regret and wanting an answer.)*

HENRY. I'm Mildred's uncle. My wife and Mildred's mother are sisters. I don't know how much you know Mildred's family, but-

MAYOLA. *(urgently)* I know them all. I have had dinner with Mr. and Mrs. Griffin. I taught the twins, Delma and Thelma, and little Robert.

HENRY. Well, Mildred's story is the white folks killed all of them. She ran and hid under the bed when they busted in the house. After it was over, she shook everybody and they all was dead. This lady, Jean took to her when she was running in the streets. Let me help Helen. This whole thing is a tragedy.

*(**MAYOLA** stands with the others in shock. **HENRY** walks offstage.)*

MAYOLA. Poor baby.

(The lights fade.)

End of Scene 1

Scene Two

*(The morning of June 12, 1921 around 10:00 a.m. **HENRY** is working on building some stairs. **HELEN** comes out of the tent carrying a basket of clothes. **HENRY** stops and notices her with the basket.)*

HENRY. Mrs. Tate is sure kind. I saw you with those two pillow cases full of clothes. Mighty kind of her and Mr. Tate to help us in our time of need.

HELEN. Mighty kind, huh?

HENRY. I guess it could be worse.

HELEN. I guess it could. But you know something?

HENRY. What's that?

HELEN. You know that pretty blue dress that my niece Leigh made for me to wear on our 20th anniversary party?

HENRY. Yes, today is June 7th, our 20th wedding anniversary. How could I forget? Leigh made that dress for you as a present. I remember how you was not going to let me see you in it until the night of the party. I know it probably got burned up like everything else. Well, we can't have no big party like we planned, but we sure got each other. I am just grateful that we are together.

HELEN. Well, it looks like this evening, I will get to show you something anyway. Look what I got.

(She pulls the blue dress out of the basket.)

HENRY. How in the world?

HELEN. I just so happened to be cleaning us Mrs. Tate's closet and low and behold, there was my dress. Still got Leigh's writing on it and says Aunt H.

HENRY. I wonder what else they got?

HELEN. Everything that's in those two pillow cases, I brought home. And, If I would've had time, I'd a got some of my other stuff.

HENRY. Boy! It's hard to trust white folks ain't it.

*(**HELEN** looks at **HENRY** with a matter of fact face as she starts towards the wash bucket. She starts to take the rest of the clothes out of the pillow case as **MILDRED***

comes out of the tent with another basket and walks over to **HELEN**. **OLA FAYE** *and* **CHARLES** *enter with a wagon each that include supplies. They walk over to* **HENRY** *as* **HELEN** *and* **MILDRED** *come forward.)*

OLA FAYE. How are you doing sir!

HENRY. Hello to you Miss Ola Faye and Mr. Charles, sir. What can we do for you both?

CHARLES. Good to see all three of you again? How is young Mildred?

MILDRED. Fine. Thank you.

HELEN. Hello. It is good to see you all again. How is everything at the hospital?

OLA FAYE. Things are getting better. I mean, it is a little slower. We have been trying to transition people back to their homes, which we know are not in the best condition right now. The Red Cross has really been working hard to make sure people get the supplies they need to get through all of this. Mr. Maurice Willows is making sure that the National Red Cross Headquarters is working hard to make sure this transition is helpful.

HENRY. Well, you tell Mr. Willows that we definitely appreciate all the help. This here tent is better than nothing. And believe me the supplies come in handy.

CHARLES. Speaking of supplies we came to deliver both of these wagons to you and your family. We also came to check in on Miss Helen and little Miss Mildred to see how they were doing.

MILDRED. Sometimes my feet hurt, but I can still walk okay.

HELEN. I am fine. Every now and then, I might get a slight headache, but the medicine you all gave me seems to help.

OLA FAYE. That's good. I made sure that we brought you some more, in case you start to run out. And just know, if you all need anything else, come by the school. We will be there for a little while longer. They are talking about moving us to a smaller location, but we want to do all we can to help you.

HENRY. Thank you, Miss Ola Faye and Mr. Charles. When we get back on our feet, we would love to have the both of you join us for dinner. The wife makes some mean fried chicken.

OLA FAYE. Thank you. It sounds like a lovely idea.

CHARLES. Much obliged. We will see you all soon.

(*CHARLES and* **OLA FAYE** *walk away stage right and run into* **MAYOLA.** *They talk to each other and give pleasant exchanges during the following scene with* **HELEN** *and* **MILDRED.**)

HELEN. Mildred, grab one of those wagons and bring it in the tent.

MILDRED. Yes, ma'am.

HELEN. *(To* **MILDRED***)* You make some room over there for this stuff and start putting it on the table. I will be right back.

(**MILDRED** *grabs a handle on the wagon and takes it into the tent. As* **MILDRED** *gets into the tent with* **HELEN** *following behind her,* **HELEN** *and* **HENRY** *notice* **MAYOLA** *talking to* **CHARLES** *and* **OLA FAYE***, but go on about their business as the scene cross fades to stage right.)*

MAYOLA. I want to thank you Miss Ola Faye and Mr. Charles for all of your help at the hospital.

OLA FAYE. That's why we are here Miss Mayola.

MAYOLA. You both know, I'm still looking for my son.

CHARLES. Yes, ma'am.

MAYOLA. Well, I got some good news the other day that he is alive.

OLA FAYE. That is exciting ma'am. Praise God! How is he doing?

(**MAYOLA** *starts crying.)*

MAYOLA. (crying) That's just it! I know he's alive, but no one has seen him. See, little Mildred and Jesse are classmates. She says she saw him go with a man in an army uniform at one of them camps they were keeping Negroes in. Problem is that when I went to where they might have been holding him, he was nowhere to be found. I have looked all over town and I have not been able to find him. I went to the other camps, went by these tents, the hospitals, churches, everywhere. I just want to ask the both you to let me know if you see a young boy about nine years old. Mildred said his arm was wrapped up the last time she saw him.

OLA FAYE. Okay ma'am. We will do everything in our power to try to find your son.

MAYOLA. Thank you so much!

CHARLES. What did you say his name was?

MAYOLA. Jesse. Jesse Anderson. Here, please take this hand bill.

(MAYOLA gives CHARLES a handbill.)

CHARLES. Thank you, ma'am. I will definitely keep my eyes open.

MAYOLA. Thank you, sir!

OLA FAYE. You have a blessed day Miss Anderson.

(CHARLES and OLA FAYE exit right. The lights cross fade to HELEN and HENRY as MAYOLA walks to their tent.)

MAYOLA. Mr. Henry, Miss Helen. I hope I am not imposing on you.

HENRY. No ma'am. Come on over. Have a seat.

(HENRY motions to a chair.)

HELEN. Nice to see you again, Miss Anderson. What can we do for you?

MAYOLA. Well, you know I'm still searching for my boy.

HELEN. Yes, ma'am. You a strong woman Miss Anderson. It's got to be hard on you. I mean, not knowing where he be.

MAYOLA. Yes, ma'am. I haven't been able to have much peace at all during this time. I guess the hard part is not knowing where he is now. But, Mildred, she really helped me. My heart started beating hard when she said she saw him alive. Is she doing all right?

HELEN. She's doing fine. As long as I keep her busy. The child likes to sing though. The way she's going, she might be able to teach me a whole lot of new church songs. She is wearing me out with some of them hymns.

MAYOLA. Sorry. Ms. Helen, I did not know about Mildred's *(beat)* experience.

HELEN. It's okay Mrs. Anderson, Mildred is a strong little girl. She will be all right.

MAYOLA. Well, E.W. Woods is trying to pull all the teachers together. We have a meeting set up at First Baptist next week. We are supposed to figure out how we're going to start educating our children again. That Mildred is a real smart girl, I'm sure she will be ready to learn.

HENRY. Yes, ma'am.

MAYOLA. But, Mr. Henry and Miss Helen, I don't want to impose upon you and in this case impose upon Mildred, because she been through so much. But, I was hoping that you would allow me to ask Mildred a few more questions about when she saw Jesse.

(HENRY and HELEN look at each other.)

MAYOLA. *(continues)* I promise, I will not upset her or cause her to think about her pain, it's just that she is the only one that I know who knows Jesse is alive. It might be something to trigger her memory on who took him or where he might be. Please, let me talk to her. I promise, I promise if I say something wrong that upsets her, I won't say anything else. I am just so desperate. I need to find my baby. I need to find my son.

(MAYOLA starts crying. She takes out a handkerchief from her purse as HELEN and HENRY look at each other. HELEN nods "yes" to HENRY.)

HENRY. *(calling)* Mildred!

(MILDRED comes out of the tent.)

MILDRED. Yes sir!

HENRY. Mrs. Anderson is here to talk to you.

(MILDRED sees MAYOLA.)

MILDRED. Hi Mrs. Anderson.

MAYOLA. Hi Mildred. How are you doing?

MILDRED. Fine. Are you still going to be my teacher next year?

MAYOLA. I hope so Mildred.

MILDRED. That's good! I like school. I wish we had school in the summer.

MAYOLA. You are a good student Mildred! Mildred?

MILDRED. Ma'am?

MAYOLA. I want to ask you a few questions about that day you saw Jesse.

MILDRED. He was holding his arm and trying to eat a bologna sandwich.

MAYOLA. What else did you and Jesse talk about?

161

MILDRED. He asked me about Robert. And I told him Robert was-was you know, dead.

MAYOLA. I am so sorry to hear that Mildred.

MILDRED. Jesse was sad too. He said he did not know where you were. He asked me if I saw you. I told him, I didn't. He said that you might be, *(beat)* dead.

MAYOLA. Did he say where they were taking him?

MILDRED. No ma'am. He just say something about going with the army folks because of his daddy, you know, dead in the army.

MAYOLA. Going with the army folks?

MILDRED. Yes'm.

MAYOLA. Did he say anything else?

MILDRED. Not that I can remember.

MAYOLA. Thank you, Mildred! Thank you so much!

MILDRED. Mrs. Anderson?

MAYOLA. Yes, Mildred?

MILDRED. Thank you for being my teacher!

MAYOLA. You are so welcome baby!

(**MAYOLA** *gives* **MILDRED** *a big hug as the lights fade.*)

End of Scene Two

Scene Three

(June 13, 1921 10:00 a.m. The tent of the law offices of Franklin, Spears and Chappelle. Milton is sitting at a table reading. Jacob and Leaudra enter. Milton stands and shakes Jacob's hand. Jacob pulls out a chair for Leaudra who sits.)

JACOB. What is wrong with these white folks? Why do they consistently say one thing, and then do another?

MILTON. Are you talking about the City of Tulsa reporting that they will support the Negro Community and help its fine citizens to rebuild and then thwart every opportunity for them to do so?

JACOB. Exactly.

LEAUDRA. What is going on with this fire ordinance situation? We are trying to rebuild our homes and our businesses. Is Buck Franklin, Spears and Chappelle making any progress with our cause? It seems like things are moving slow.

MILTON. Sometimes these things take time.

JACOB. It didn't take no time for the white folks to come in here and steal all of our stuff, shoot us in the back and burn our livelihood and homes down. It took them less than eighteen hours. So how long should it take them to give it back?

LEAUDRA. And what is the message from the insurance companies?

MILTON. Well the Grand Jury said-

LEAUDRA. To hell with the all-white Grand Jury-

MILTON. See, Gurley's statement-

LEAUDRA. To hell with Gurley! Hell, he's gone. He ain't no leader. I ain't never heard the people say he was leading them.

JACOB. We just want justice! We need to go outside of this Tulsa Community and get justice. The leaders we got in this community ain't worth a damn. Where is all the support from the National Urban League and the NAACP? They said that they are giving us support in thousands of dollars. Where is that money going?

MILTON. I don't know sir. We do not know where they are sending that money.

LEAUDRA. What you mean you don't know?

MILTON. As far as we know it is going through the proper channels.

LEAUDRA. Through the proper channels of the white folks? So anytime somebody tries to help this community or do something to support it, the money has to go to the white folks. This sound like a bunch of ignorant, low-life, shiesty leadership to me. Now, I know these lawyers mean well, but something seems phony.

MILTON. Ma'am, I assure you that Franklin, Spears and Chappelle are doing all they can-

LEAUDRA. I ain't talking about them. These white folks are keeping that money one way or another. The only real help I see, is coming from the Red Cross.

MILTON. Ma'am the NAACP made a large contribution for legal work and relief for our Negro citizens. And I guarantee you that those things cost a lot of money for us to stop the fire ordinance. I mean there were legal fees, court costs, travel, and all kinds of things that contributed to that ordinance being stopped.

JACOB. We understand that, but where is the lumber so we can build our house? Where is the brick and mortar to build a fire place? Where is the money needed to rebuild? How long do we have to live in these tents? Winter is coming, and we have got to survive. I know, I told one of them white commissioners the other day, when he asked me what I was going to do and I told him that I was going to start over right here in Tulsa where I started before. This is my land, and I can do what I want to do with it. I just need a little money to get the supplies.

MILTON. Mr. Jacob, we are doing all we can to-

LEAUDRA. It ain't good enough! We got to get out here and bust our asses to make this thing work! Negroes can't sit around here waiting on the white man to have some kind of conscience and save us! We got to get off our asses and save ourselves. We want to know, will you and them lawyers help us to organize our own and rebuild?

MILTON. I am positive that the law firm of Chappelle, Spears and Franklin will work hard to pull the Negro community together to rebuild.

JACOB. The community is organizing a meeting to discuss what we are going to do for ourselves next week. Hopefully, somebody from this law firm will be there to support what we plan to do.

MILTON. I assure you we will be there. Mr. Jacob, did you ever find or get to talk to A.J. Smitherman? What about John Williams? Have you heard anything from O.B. Mann?

JACOB. All I know is they are either hiding out or like my friend Samuel, they left Tulsa like Gurley in fear of their lives and will probably never return. But, the situation is that we are still here. What is left of our families is still here. Those men fought hard for their beliefs whether you agree or disagree. Many of our people in this community put their

164

lives on the line for us to continue to live the way we live. Not only did men die, but our innocent women and children died too. I don't care how much money goes to legal fees or how much money goes to help our people, the truth of the matter is we can't keep sitting around here waiting for these white folks to give us some help.

LEAUDRA. He's telling you right son. White folks didn't help us build this community. They left us alone and we built it ourselves. They left us alone too much and they realized that in many cases we were living better than them. Ooo, if you want to make the white boy respect you, don't ask him for nothing. Do it yourself. So, what? He might feel threatened, that's because you're demonstrating to him that you just as smart as he is. Son, you got to learn to play the game. As long as he thinks you need him, he going to do all he can to tear you down. But, when you are bold and strong and stand up on your own two feet, you rise up and become a threat to him. And he will do all he can to tear you down. The first thing he will do is try to get your own people to turn against you. Listen to me boy! 'Cause you got them colored fools out there who believe everything that white boy tells them. And you see them every day. Watch 'em they easy to spot. Always grinning and shining. Might as well, be slaves! Jacob! I'm through here. Let's get on about our business!

(LEAUDRA rises and JACOB follows her as they exit.)

MILTON. Thanks for coming by.

(The lights fade to black.)

End of Scene Three

Scene Four

(June 13, 1921 at 5:00 p.m. **HENRY** *is adjusting the bottom of the tent. He stands back and looks at the top and walks around the upstage area of the tent and back around it. As he comes to the front of the tent he notices* **JACOB** *and* **LEAUDRA** *enter his area.)*

HENRY. Jacob, Mrs. Harris. What can I do for you?

JACOB. Evening Henry.

LEAUDRA. Henry.

JACOB. How's Helen and the little girl doing?

HENRY. They're fine. Helen is at the Tate's and she took Mildred with her today to show her how to do some of the cleaning and ironing.

LEAUDRA. Yes. You got to start them young. Makes them appreciate things a little better when they get older.

HENRY. Yes ma'am.

JACOB. Well, Henry. We appreciate what you said in the church meeting last night about how we need to rebuild as soon as possible. We agree with you.

HENRY. Well, I only said what needed to be said.

LEAUDRA. Yes. We just left the law offices of Franklin, Spears and Chappelle.

HENRY. Seems like those lawyers are working in our best interests.

JACOB. They are doing what they can, but it is not enough. We as a people need to do more.

HENRY. That's what I was saying. We need to pull together and rebuild. We need to help each other one by one until we build this community back up.

JACOB. I agree with you Henry, but when we rebuild it, we have got to make sure that the white folks don't turn around and burn it down to the ground.

HENRY. I don't think they will do that Jacob.

JACOB. What you mean, Henry? These white folks don't even want us to rebuild. If we are going to do this, we need to make sure that this won't happen anymore. We just can't take their word for it.

HENRY. That's all a man has is his word.

LEAUDRA. And white boys words ain't worth the mouth it come out of.

HENRY. Remember when Booker T. Washington came to the Dreamland Theatre?

LEAUDRA. How could we forget? It was so many Negroes there, folks was standing outside.

HENRY. Me and Helen was on the front row. One of the things that I liked about what Booker T. said was that as Negroes, we are going to run into discrimination from white folks. That's just going to be a way of life.

JACOB. Of course. I agree with him on that.

HENRY. He talked about how we need to help ourselves. We need to concentrate on hard work and helping ourselves in spite of the difficulty. White folks are going to hate us. Ain't nothing we can do about that. We have just got to look over that and work hard every day.

JACOB. So, what do we do about it?

HENRY. I am like Booker T. That is the only way that white folks will respect us. After we get the white folks to respect us, they will accept us in today's society.

JACOB. I get what Booker T. was talking about. I do. But, with all his talk about Greenwood being the Negro Wall Street, the white folks did not respect that.

HENRY. What are you saying Jacob?

JACOB. We had all kinds of businesses, homes, rental properties and what did they do? Instead of respecting us. They got jealous and mad. They felt like we Negroes were uppity. They didn't like us living the way we were living. Now, they want to make sure, that it never happens again. That's why we need to rebuild, but we need to have a different way of thinking.

HENRY. What kind of way are you thinking Jacob?

JACOB. Well, you remember when W.E.B. Dubois came to the Dreamland Theatre a few years ago?

LEAUDRA. Another time that the Dreamland was so full, folks was hanging out the rafters.

HENRY. I was there. I wasn't on the front row, but I was close. Helen and I have always been the type of folks to want to know what our leaders is thinking.

JACOB. I understand W.E. B. I still got the handbill that I keep in my wallet.

HENRY. Man! How you always keeping up with stuff like that.

JACOB. I like this quote that was on the handbill.

(JACOB pulls out a folded handbill from his wallet.)

JACOB. *(continues and reading.)* Look what he says, "The Negro Race, like all races, is going to be saved by its exceptional men. The problem of education then, among Negroes must first of all deal with the "Talented Tenth."

HENRY. Yes, I remember him talking about the "Talented Tenth."

JACOB. It is the problem of developing the best of this race that they may guide the mass away from contamination and death of the worst."

HENRY. Well, it don't look like A.J. Smitherman, John Williams and O.B. Mann got us away from death. Looks like their leadership is what got us in this situation in the first place. They couldn't be a part of the Talented Tenth."

LEAUDRA. Sounds like Henry got a point Jacob?

JACOB. I did not say that those men were a part of the Talented Tenth. They were only trying to make a buck like the rest of our so-called Negro leaders. We need strong leadership.

HENRY. Well, who do you suggest we get?

JACOB. We need people that are willing to make sure that when we rebuild they do not find legal clauses to take our land away from us. We also need people who are going to be willing to take some heat from white folks. We, as a community must protect our leaders and their families from harm's way. Hopefully, Franklin, Spears and Chappelle might step up. As well as educators like E.W. Woods.

HENRY. Booker T. and W.E.B. talked about the same thing. They want us colored folks to work for ourselves. I don't even know why we are arguing about this point.

JACOB. Yes. They want the same thing. But, the strategies of getting the same thing are so different. Booker T. wants us to work hard, build houses, work for the white folks and save our money.

HENRY. Sounds like a good plan to me. Sounds like the plan that I am going to do.

JACOB. No Henry! Dubois says we got to have a seat at the table.

HENRY. What do I want to sit at the white man's table for?

JACOB. That's why these lawyers are so important. We have got to sit at the table and make the same rules and laws that the white folks have. If we do not have a seat at the table and get our civil rights then we are doomed to let history repeat itself.

HENRY. I don't think the white folks is gon' to do what they just did again.

JACOB. They might not do it this way, but what's to say that they won't find another way of destroying the community that we rebuild. We have got to be more progressive instead of so passive.

HENRY. I just don't think we should waste our time fighting for civil rights when there are so many opportunities to make a living. It don't matter to me whether it is being a butler or shining shoes, money is money.

JACOB. Now, that's where you are wrong Henry.

HENRY. How can that be wrong? I am putting two kids through college right now from the money I have made working for white folks.

JACOB. But, don't you understand Henry! You're putting your children through college so they can have the education that you didn't have. They are learning how important it is to study philosophy, Greek and Latin. Those schools are teaching them how to fight for civil rights.

HENRY. That school is also teaching them how to make a living. One of them plan to be a doctor and the other one wants to be a teacher. As long as they can make a good living and do better than I did, it don't really matter to me.

JACOB. But what if they end up like Dr. Jackson. He worked hard and got all that education and what good did it do, when this young white boy shot him in the back and killed him. And on top of all of that, no justice. We have got to listen to Dubois and fight back and gain true rights.

HENRY. Jacob, I think you are making this thing out of more than it is. As far as I am concerned, our community needs to rebuild and never even mention what happened. You know sometimes it is best to leave well enough alone.

JACOB. Never even mention it? You mean just be silent and go on like nothing has ever happened? That is crazy. That is passive. That would be a big problem for many years to come. We cannot sit still and do nothing! Why do we have to be so ignorant? Come on Henry! Stand up for yourself and what you believe.

HENRY. Look Jacob. It ain't my fight. I am too old. You go ahead and fight for your civil rights and see how far it gets you. I don't agree with all that stuff. For me, I am going to support anybody who wants to rebuild and move on. Anything more than that, I will not have time.

JACOB. Man! It's Negroes like you that let the white man know that we continue to disrespect ourselves and our people.

HENRY. Do you need anything else? If not, I got work to do.

JACOB. I guess not. All right Mamadea', it looks like Henry is one of those Negroes who will never see the true meaning of what colored folks need to do. Henry, I'm sorry to say this, but it is Negroes like you with no guts, no balls and no courage to stand up for what is right.

HENRY. I'm sorry you feel that way Jacob. I just think you are being hot-headed and wasting your time trying to make the white folks do something for you.

JACOB. You deserve whatever the white man does to you. I don't know if I will continue to stay here in Tulsa with this madness. I am starting to realize why a lot of people are leaving this town. Take care, Henry.

HENRY. Have a good evening Jacob. Mrs. Harris.

LEAUDRA. Henry.

(**JACOB** *and* **LEAUDRA** *leave as the lights fade.*)

End of Scene Four

Scene 5

(June 14, 1921 8:00 a.m. **HENRY** *and* **HELEN** *are sitting outside of their tent. They are both drinking a cup of coffee.* **MILDRED** *is playing in the yard with a jump rope.)*

HELEN. I am sure glad you kept that money in the Boley bank. We got a pretty good savings and we might be able to build our house back with it.

HENRY. I know Helen. I have been thinking about what we might need to do since the insurance money didn't work out.

HELEN. Well, I've been thinking too.

HENRY. What you thinking about Helen?

HELEN. How long are we both gon' keep working for the Bradys.

HENRY. What are you talking about Helen?

HELEN. With this uprising, we finally see the type of people they are. Everybody say that Mr. Brady is with the Klan. You even say he was wrong for supporting that fire ordinance. And, I can't believe Mrs. Brady had the nerve to come in my house and take my stuff.

HENRY. You don't know that for sure Helen.

HELEN. Well, if she didn't, she didn't go buy it at the store. She knowed it came from colored folks. I wish I would have caught her wearing my blue dress. I'd of-

HENRY. Stayed in your place and not do nothing.

HELEN. That's what I am saying Henry! Things is different now. And times have changed.

HENRY. What has changed Helen?

HELEN. Look around you. Today is Thursday. Thursday used to be the day when I would go shopping for us. I would talk to Ms. Little and the other ladies at the hairdresser. Then, you and I would stop by and talk to my sister Mattie and Leigh at the seamstress shop. Then, we would go to the Dreamland Theatre together and watch a picture show.

HENRY. I understand what you're saying dear. We worked hard to make a living and raise a family and it was those glorious times on Greenwood that I miss too.

*(***HENRY** *chuckles as he reminisces.)*

HENRY. *(continues)* I remember at Vadel's Pool Hall old Willie Connor was talking noise about how he was the best pool shark on Greenwood. He was beating everybody at 25 cents a whop! Then at the Carter's Barber shop you talking about a whole lot of mess talking. I ain't heard so many colored men lying so much in my life. And the funny thing about it; it's the same colored men that serve on the Deacon Boards in all the churches on this side of the tracks in Tulsa.

HELEN. See Henry, that's what I mean. Why come we can't get back what we had and more?

HENRY. We can Helen, honey. We gon' rebuild this house.

HELEN. I was thinking that not only can we rebuild this house, but we can rebuild Greenwood.

HENRY. What are you saying Helen?

HELEN. How long we been working for the Bradys?

HENRY. About ten years, I reckon.

HELEN. Ten years of washing Mr. Brady's clothes and ironing his shirts. Ten years of fixing his breakfast and serving his family dinner. Ten years of washing his car and driving him to work. Ten years-

HENRY. Ten years! Yes, Helen ten years! What are you trying to say?

HELEN. I would like to spend the next ten years working for us. We could start our own business. If we gon' rebuild our home, then we need to rebuild Greenwood too. It's what we know Henry. A lot of colored folks didn't put they money in them white folks bank, but we did. And God in all his mercy see fit for us to get it all back. I knows it ain't nothing but a few hundred dollars, but it's enough for us to start a new business. Folks gon' still need stuff and folks gon' get it somewhere. My mama taught me and Mattie how to sew. I can pick up where she left off. I can cook real good. You, yourself done talked about how I make the best fried chicken in town. And, you, you have always been good at taking care of cars. You could start your own jitney service. People always looking for a ride. Or as much as you tinkered with Mr. Bradys cars you could fix people's cars. We could open any business we want to Henry. Or we can go back to working for the Bradys. You the man of the house. It is your decision.

HENRY. That's what this is all about ain't it. You don't want to keep working for the Bradys. You know I was just talking to Jacob and Mrs. Harris about what Booker T. Washington said we should do. He said that we should not worry about all this discrimination and work for yourself or folks like the Bradys. Jim Crow is gon' be here for good. I always got the part about building your own house, I guess I never did think about starting your own business. But, what about making more money with the Bradys?

HELEN. I'm sorry. I don't want to work for the Bradys no more. I am really having a hard time with it.

172

HENRY. But, Helen it is good money. The Bradys have been paying us well above what the average colored folks make for doing what we do?

HELEN. I know Henry, it's just that-I-I remembered what happened to me the night. And, I ain't said nothing to nobody, but now that I remember, every time I go to that Brady house, I get a strange feeling like I want to do something to them. It tears me up inside Henry. It just tears me up that we could work for somebody that is so mean.

HENRY. My Lord Helen. What do you remember?

HELEN. It's what I seen and heard that scares me. I might not even should be alive.

HENRY. Tell me Helen, please.

HELEN. Well, that night of the uprising, I was in my maid quarters as usual. I was about to turn in for the night. Then, I hear Mr. Brady come in the house. Then, I hear him fussing at Mrs. Brady about how we need to kill all the niggers. He said that Bradys ain't about to let niggers, kill whites. He told her about colored folks shooting white folks at the court house. He said that he was gon' kill all black folks in his sight, starting with the ones he had working for him. I got worried when I heard Mrs. Brady say, "Kill the Bastards." She told him that I was in my maid quarters and he could start with me. I ran down the back stairs and into the woods and he was shooting at me. He was calling my name. I just knew I was running fast and hard. I remember falling and that's it. It seems like it all just blacks out. Since I been back to work it is hard for Mrs. Brady to look at me. She talks to me with her back to me or she looks past me. Mr. Brady glares at me like he still wants to kill me. It's just so hard for me Henry.

*(**HELEN** starts crying.)*

HELEN. *(continues)* I know that we need the money. I know we are trying to rebuild. I still hope we can get the insurance money, but I am just having a hard time.

HENRY. It's okay Helen. It's okay. I have been noticing a change in Mr. Brady too. We don't have to go back there no more. We got enough to make it. We might not be able to send much to our kids for a while, but we will press through it. Plus, we got to take care of Mildred. We got to raise her right and make sure she gets a good education.

HELEN. Oh, Henry. I am glad you understand. But, I know that if we will work for ourselves as hard as we work for the Bradys, we will make ends meet.

HENRY. Helen, my dear. We won't just make ends meet, with the help of God we will become successful business folks. Come here and give me a hug.

*(**HENRY** and **HELEN** hug as the lights fade.)*

End of Scene Five

Scene 6

(June 21, 1921 10:00 a.m. It is a week later in the morning at the tent of Franklin, Spears and Chappelle. **MILTON** *is sitting at the table writing in a tablet.* **MAYOLA** *enters and extends her hand.)*

MAYOLA. How are you doing sir?

MILTON. Miss Mayola. What can I do for you today?

MAYOLA. You know I have been looking for my boy.

MILTON. Yes, ma'am. I hope you find him. I'm sure that everybody who knows you is also looking out for signs of your son.

MAYOLA. Well, I got a chance to talk to little Mildred with the Johnsons. And she gave me some more information and I was trying to see if I could get some legal help to see if I can find my boy. She said that he went with the army man. I was wondering if you could ask the lawyers if they could check with the army and see if my boy is with them.

MILTON. Well, I can check with Mr. Chappelle. He is the one that is more familiar with the armed forces. I am sure he will tell me that he can't promise anything.

MAYOLA. I know it's a long shot, but if he can at least try. Here, I made this handbill that has all the information.

MILTON. Is it the same handbill you have been passing out? If so, I got a couple all ready.

MAYOLA. Do I need to fill out anything for my request?

MILTON. No ma'am. I know that all three attorneys are aware of this situation. I will make sure that Mr. Chappelle gets the handbill and ask him to make your request to the army. Again, we can't promise nothing, but we will do what we can.

MAYOLA. Thank you, sir.

*(***MAYOLA*** turns to leave and sees* **HENRY** *and* **HELEN***.)*

HELEN. Miss Anderson. It is so nice to see you.

MAYOLA. Mr. and Mrs. Johnson, what a coincidence. I have been working so hard to find my son. I went to the army folks and they just gave me the run-a-round. I thought maybe if I went to a lawyer they might at least check and see what happened to my boy.

HENRY. We are praying that you find him Ms. Anderson.

MAYOLA. How's Mildred?

HELEN. She is fine. Says she can't wait for school to start.

MAYOLA. That's good! You both have a good day.

HENRY. You too.

(*MAYOLA exists as* **HELEN** *and* **HELEN** *walk over to* **MILTON**.)

MILTON. Mr. and Mrs. Johnson what can I do for you?

HENRY. We are here to see about how we start a business.

MILTON. You mean you are going to stop working for the Bradys?

HENRY. Yes sir.

MILTON. Congratulations! What is Mr. Brady going to do without you?

HENRY. I'm sure he'll find someone else. And, with my wife Helen working in the kitchen of our new restaurant, Mrs. Brady will have to look for some new help too.

MILTON. Well, good luck to the both of you? You know the future looks pretty good. I mean, despite the uprising, some people may not be able to rebuild as fast, but I am sure you can get a proper establishment in a few months.

HELEN. Yes, we were going to start by cooking Saturday and Sunday dinners. Henry will be working on us building a new kitchen before we even build the house. We already have several people ordering dinners.

MILTON. We have been getting a lot of requests for people wanting to rebuild or start new businesses. I have an application packet ready. If you all can fill this information out and bring it back to me when you are ready, I can get everything going for you. In the meantime, if you need any help completing the packet, please let me know. Also, put me on that list for one of those chicken dinners for Saturday and Sunday.

HENRY. We sure will. Thank you, sir.

HELEN. Good bye!

(**HELEN** *and* **HENRY** *exit.* **OLA FAYE** *and* **CHARLES** *enter from the other direction.*)

CHARLES. Hey, Mr. Lawyer.

MILTON. How are you Mr. Doctor?

CHARLES. Trying to learn as much as I can.

MILTON. You'll get there. Especially, when you got this pretty lady helping you. How are you Miss Ola Faye.

OLA FAYE. I am doing fine, sir.

MILTON. What can I do for the both of you today?

CHARLES. Well, we are both new to this and we wanted to find out what we needed to do to get a marriage license?

MILTON. Congratulations! All you need to do is jump the broom!

OLA FAYE. Jump the broom?

MILTON. Just joking around. Both of you all sit down and fill this out and I will explain what you need to do. Getting married! That is all right! Boy! It has been a busy day!

(**CHARLES** and **OLA FAYE** *happily sit down as* **CHARLES** *pulls a chair out for her as the lights fade.*)

End of Scene Six

Scene 7

(Outside of the Johnson's tent on June 25, 1921 1:00 p.m. **HELEN** *is coming in and out of a second tent with prepared dinners wrapped in wax paper and paper plates. She is sitting those prepared dinners on the table.* **MILDRED** *picks up two dinners and takes them to* **LEAUDRA** *and* **JACOB** *who are sitting at a card table with two chairs.* **HENRY** *is cleaning another table and putting stuff in a trash can.* **MAYOLA** *is eating a dinner at another table.* **MILTON** *enters and walks over to* **HENRY**.*)

MILTON. Mr. Henry. I am here. I can't wait to wrap my fingers around some of your wife's fried chicken.

HENRY. Good to see you, sir. Mr. Milton's here! Can you get his order ready?

HELEN. Coming up!

HENRY. Boy! It has really been busy today. I was up early getting them chickens ready. We can already see that this this is going so well we are going to have to work faster and harder.

MILTON. Well, here is my dollar! Keep the change.

*(**HENRY** takes the dollar and writes something on a small pad.)*

HENRY. Why thank you Mr. Milton. This twenty-five cents tip will help us get some chicken feed.

MILTON. We got to support each other Mr. Henry. You and your wife are just a seed for getting this community back on its feet.

HENRY. Thank you, sir. I just cleaned this table off so, you can sit here.

*(**MILTON** sits down and **JACOB** waves for **HENRY** to come to him.)*

JACOB. Henry.

HENRY. What can I do for you Mr. Jacob?

JACOB. Henry. You tell Helen, that we ain't had fried chicken like this in so long that she is going to have to have you raise a whole new bunch of yard birds before next Saturday.

*(**JACOB** and **HENRY** start laughing.)*

HENRY. It's okay with me. We just appreciate the church and everybody helping us get

177

started. I know we don't have it all together yet, but folks are starting to come out the woodworks. Helen said if folks keep coming we may run out.

LEAUDRA. Well, before you do, Jacob, buy two more dinners for us to go.

HENRY. Yes ma'am.

(*JACOB gives* **HENRY** *one dollar and fifty cents.*)

JACOB. Here you go sir.

(**MILDRED** *takes* **MILTON** *a plate.*)

HENRY. Let me tell Helen to make sure she saves y'all two plates to go.

(**HENRY** *walks in the tent where* **HELEN** *is fixing dinners.* **CHARLES** *and* **OLA FAYE** *walk into the area where there are tables and chairs.*)

CHARLES. Good afternoon everybody! Good afternoon! Today is a very special day for a lot of people. But, I must be selfish and talk about myself first! I am now the proud husband of Mrs. Ola Faye Cherry. Can we get a round of applause?

(*Everyone starts clapping as* **HENRY** *and* **HELEN** *walk out to see what is going on.*)

CHARLES. (*continues*) And there they are. I would also like to say thank you to one of our new upcoming businesses in the community. I don't know the name of it yet, but I know I could smell Miss Helen's Fried Chicken two blocks away!

(*Everyone laughs and cheers for Miss* **HELEN** *and* **HENRY**.)

CHARLES. (*continues*) Miss Helen and Mr. Henry, thank you for helping to bring resilient spirit to this community back alive. Let's give them both a round of applause.

(*Everyone claps and cheers.*)

CHARLES. (*continues*) Now my next announcement comes without words.

(**CHARLES** *whistles.* **JESSE** *enter from stage left.* **MAYOLA** *takes a few steps towards* **JESSE** *and he runs to her. They both meet center stage and give each other a hug.* **MAYOLA** *is careful not to hug* **JESSE** *too hard on his bandaged shoulder. The entire congregation stops as they witness this reunion.* **MILDRED** *walks over and* **MAYOLA** *hugs* **MILDRED**.)

JACOB. Well, Mamadea', I guess this is just about a good time as any.

LEAUDRA. Are you sure you are ready to do this son?

JACOB. Mamadea', you know how I feel. I-I thought about it a lot. And, I-I just don't think I can do it anymore. Ain't no sense in wasting no more time.

LEAUDRA. Do what you must do son.

(JACOB stands up and walks upstage center. LEAUDRA stands and steps to the side and stays downstage. JACOB raises his hand.)

JACOB. Can I get everyone's attention? Can I please get everyone's attention?

(The crowd slowly gets quiet and everyone looks at JACOB.)

JACOB. *(continues)* I too, have an announcement to make. But, before I make this announcement, I got to say what I got to say. It's a hard thing to say right now, and some of y'all know me enough to know that I speak from my heart, whether you like it or not.

(JACOB pauses for a few seconds as it gets very still and quiet.)

JACOB. *(continues)* First, let me say I applaud y'all, for being resilient. I mean it's people like Henry and Helen who will help rebuild this community to be what Booker T. Washington said, "The Negro Wall Street." Henry and Helen are good people. And, y'all all know that Helen makes some mean fried chicken!

CHARLES. Yes, sir!

(Everyone smiles and laughs.)

JACOB. Yes sir. Y'all all good people. You all are working hard to bring this community back to the glorious moments of where it was a few weeks ago before the uprising. Some of y'all got visions for the future. Visions for your families, businesses, education, and religion. But, I just can't stand with you on this. I can't stand with you if the white folks don't take responsibility for what they did to us. I can't stand with you as long as they won't have to pay for what they did by murdering our innocent men, women, and children. How can we live with people who spit on us and treat us like we are animals? How can we work with people who won't demonstrate integrity and admit to their wrongs? These people lie to us, trick us out of what is rightfully ours, beat us, rape our women, lynch us, and dump us in mass graves without a decent burial, and expect us to go on as if nothing happened and keep hush-hush about it all. How can we move forward without understanding what happened?

HENRY. Jacob. You don't have to say this right now. We all know what you are saying but, it is time we move on, forget about this, and hope it will never happen again.

*(**CHARLES, OLA FAYE, HELEN, MILTON** and **MAYOLA**, nod their heads in*

agreement with **HENRY**.*)*

JACOB. See, that is my problem. You are my problem. These white folks are not going to work with us. That's why some of those men that went to that courthouse for Dick Rowland were not fighting for Dick Rowland, they were fighting for you, their families, and this community. They fought for their pride and dignity. They fought to uphold the values they worked so hard for. And, by fighting, many of them died so that you would be able to live like true men and women who could lead us into a better future. Don't you understand? By rebuilding and acting like nothing happened, it will only happen again. By not recognizing what the white folks did, you open a door for them to do it again. Rebuild this community. Stay hushed mouthed! And watch the white folks tear it up again! We need to recognize our strength. Our strength is us! We have got to stick together!

HENRY. Jacob. That's what we are doing. We are sticking together.

JACOB. Sorry, Henry. You are not. You might think you are, but you are not. Right now, we are too passive. I guess the fight in us has been beat down so bad that it is gone. I can't do it. I can't sit here and watch it. I can't be a part of it. Like the so-called leaders of this community can no longer be found, I am one of those who's looking for a new promised land. Right here, right now, there is no leadership willing to truly fight for what they destroyed. This whole thing with the white folks blaming Negroes for all of this and we are the victim astonishes me. And we can't get an official apology and must go to legal remedies to rebuild on our own land? And, they expect us to go on, remain hush-hush and act like it didn't happen. How long will we have to remain hush-hush? How long will it be before we are able to explain this to our children and our children's children? They say home is where the heart is. God knows my heart is here with you all and my family. But, my heart is heavy. It's heavy because I know the way it looks now, nothing will change. So, to keep my heart beating, I got to go. I can't stay. So, I'm leaving town.

HENRY. But Jacob, where are you going to go?

JACOB. Somewhere where I can wake up the next morning and know that I am a man!

*(**JACOB** hugs **LEAUDRA**. She squeezes him hard with tears in her eyes.)*

JACOB. *(continues)* Bye Mamadea'.

*(**JACOB** walks off as the others gaze at him. **LEAUDRA** walks slowly after him, but stops center stage. **HENRY** meets **LEAUDRA** center stage.)*

HENRY. Where do you suppose he'll go?

LEAUDRA. Don't know. But, wherever he goes, I hope he finds himself.

HENRY. Think he'll ever come back?

LEAUDRA. Not in my lifetime. Not in my lifetime

LEAUDRA. *(singing)*
Guide me O though great Jehovah
Pilgrim through this barren land

EVERYONE. *(singing)*
Guide me O though great Jehovah
Pilgrim through this barren land

> *(No one sings.* **LEAUDRA** *looks towards the area* **JACOB** *left as the lights fade to black).*

End of Scene Seven

Scene 8 (Curtain Call)

(The curtain call is a tableau. The lights should project a black and white photographic look on the stage to resemble a large picture. No one smiles. Everyone is frozen. **LEAUDRA** *is center stage looking towards the direction that* **JACOB** *left.* **JACOB** *is positioned in a turn and looking back towards* **LEAUDRA**. **HELEN, HENRY** *and* **MILDRED** *are positioned as workers downstage of the tent.* **MAYOLA** *and* **JESSE** *are in an embrace (no smiles).* **CHARLES** *and* **OLA FAYE** *are holding hands in a serious loving moment.* **MILTON** *is looking at a document.* **SAMUEL** *is seen as if he is walking away and off stage. After ten seconds to fifteen seconds the lights fade to black.)*

End of Scene Eight

End of Play

References

Cannady, M. (2015) *Back Cover Photograph of Rodney Clark.* Mr. Shorty Photography. Tulsa, OK.

Crafts, T and Finnell, A. (2008) *Terror in Tulsa – History Uncovered.* CN8: In association with FullMind. Comcast Network. United States.

Ellsworth, S. (1982) *Death in a Promised Land – The Tulsa Race Riot of 1921.* Louisiana State University Press. Baton Rouge, LA.

Frontline PBS Documentary. (1998) The Two Nations of Black America. *The Debate Between W.E.B. Dubois and Booker T. Washington.* WGBH Educational Foundation. Boston, MA.

Gates, E. F. (2003) *Riot on Greenwood – The Total Destruction of Black Wall Street.* Sunbelt Eaton. Austin, TX.

History.com Editors, Buffalo Soldiers https://www.history.com/topics/westward-expansion/buffalo-soldiers December 7, 2017

Johnson, H. (2012). *Apartheid in Indian Country – Seeing Red Over Black Disenfranchisement* Sunbelt Eaton. Austin, TX.

Johnson, H. (1998). *Black Wall Street – From Riot to Renaissance in Tulsa's Historic Greenwood District.* Eakin Press. Austin, TX.

Johnson, H. (2014). *Images of America – Tulsa's Historic Greenwood District.* Arcadia Publishing. Charleston, S.C.

Latimer, A. (2017) *Tulsa City-County Library's African-American Resource Center and the YWCA Committee for Racial Justice – The 1921 Tulsa Race Riot Kit.* Tulsa, OK.

Lynch, W. (1712,2009) *The Willie Lynch Letter: The Making of A Slave.* Createspace Independent Publisher.

Randall, D. (1969) *Booker T. and W.E.B.* Detroit Free Press. Detroit, MI.

Madigan, T. (2003) *The Burning – Massacre, Destruction, and the Tulsa Race Riot of 1921.* St. Martin's Press. New York, NY.

Nicholson, S. (1983). The *Greenwood Blues of the 1921 Race Riot.* KOCO TV-5 Alive, a Gannett Station. Oklahoma City, OK.

Oklahoma Tourism and Recreation Department (2017) *Long Road to Liberty – Oklahoma's African American History and Culture.* Oklahoma City, OK

Parish, M. (1923) *Events of the Tulsa Disaster*. Limited Edition. First Printing 2009.

Tulsa Historical Society. (1921). *A Young African-American Girl.* This photo was taken shortly after the 1921 Tulsa Race Riot. Tulsa, OK.

Weller/Grossman Productions (1999) *In Search of History- The Night Tulsa Burned.* A & E. Television Networks. New York, NY.

Yared, E. (2016) *Black Past 92nd Infantry Division (1919-1919, 1942-1945)* Retrieved from https://blackpast.org/african-american-history/92nd-infantry-division-1917-1919-1942-1945-0/

Made in the USA
Columbia, SC
01 April 2019